THE
DISAPPEARANCE OF
SUMMER SOLSTICE

THE DISAPPEARANCE OF SUMMER SOLSTICE

By

Joseph C. Taylor

ISBN 1-58500-425-1

About the Book

Summer Solstice, her friends and their families are celebrating their graduation from middle school in their favorite picnic spot, Lambs Canyon. The teenagers go on a hike while they await their evening meal. Their destination… the ten thousand-foot peak, Mt. Walamalee. A violent electric storm arises…a strange light appears. Summer's curiosity catapults her and her friends into an adventure that takes them to the farthest realms of the known universe.

Survival is their byword, and death their constant companion. Earthquake, volcanic eruption, uncontrollable disease and large beasts of prey contribute to a deadly struggle for existence. They become prisoners in the future of the Earth, unable to return to their own time. No one can save them now.

CHAPTER 1

A sudden clap of thunder startled the sleeping teenagers. Summer Solstice opened her eyes and sat up from the large boulder where she had fallen asleep. The strong wind grabbed her coal-black hair and pulled it over her eyes. Summer pushed it away, surveying the entire area. Everything had changed. The occasional soft, billowy cumulus clouds had been replaced by menacing thunderclouds, rapidly approaching them from the west. Summer's attention quickly turned to her friends. The wind howled like a lonely coyote and was beginning to disturb their peaceful slumber. Steve, Monica, Jose, Maria and Tykesha, slowly opened their eyes, startled by the darkness and foreboding that surrounded them.

Summer gazed wistfully toward the trail leading back to camp. It seemed like only a short time when they had left the camping area where their families had come to celebrate the first week of summer vacation. It was a yearly tradition. Summer and her best friends were excited about this outing because they had just graduated from the eighth grade and would enter South High School as freshmen in the fall. It signified the ending of childhood and the beginning of "adulthood".

The words of caution from Summer's parents echoed in her mind. She had dismissed their concerns because Steve was an Eagle Scout and was well qualified to lead the little group. Nevertheless, she had never seen her father so worried.

Lightning danced from cloud to cloud and to the ground. Each bolt brightly illuminated the sky and was followed by the terrifying crash of thunder. It was louder than they had ever heard before. The others were now fully awake and stared at the ominous sight before them. The sun, now at the horizon, was covered by the thunderclouds, dropping the outside temperature by almost five degrees and causing the daylight to disappear rapidly.

Summer looked at her watch and gasped. "It's almost eight-thirty. It's going to get dark soon and we'll probably get soaked going down the mountain."

The force of the gale winds was increasing and strong gusts

pushed against the youth as they got up and put on their daypacks. They steadied themselves to keep from being pushed over. A feeling of urgency filled their hearts.

Their original objective had been to hike to Mt. Walamalee, a mountain peak ten thousand feet high and only one mile away from where they now stood. They had only reached the ridge at nine thousand feet. Exhausted, they had decided to sit by a large granite boulder and eat their lunch. After lunch, they had fallen asleep in the warmth of the seventy-degree temperature.

Summer's thoughts wandered to the mountain meadow below them in Lambs Canyon where their parents awaited with a dinner fit for a king. They had promised to return by eight. Summer looked again at her watch. It was eight thirty-five. Their parents would be worried.

Coming from behind the boulder, they saw the darkened sky. Above the full moon suddenly appeared in a small area of clearing in the clouds, then disappeared behind the fast-moving clouds. The static electricity in the air began to increase causing the hair on their heads and necks to be attracted toward the sky. Without warning, a large bolt of lightning pierced the air and struck the ground not more than fifty yards from the little group. The force of the electrons and instantaneous bark of thunder jolted the ground. A deafening shock wave instantly hit their ears, sending fear into their hearts. The potential danger to their lives was far too obvious. Without looking back, they quickly descended from the ridge.

After descending only a hundred yards, the wind unexpectedly stopped. The creaking of the tree trunks bending under the force of the wind and the hissing of the moving leaves disappeared. There was complete stillness and silence. Steve, who led the group, halted and the others instinctively paused at the same time. They looked around them to see what was happening. An eerie red-blue glow lit up the trees in front of them. They quickly turned around in an attempt to discover the source of the unusual light. It seemed to come from somewhere behind the large granite boulder where they had rested.

"Let's check it out", Summer blurted out as she started back toward the ridge. None of her friends moved. They stood frozen in fear of the unknown light and refused to follow. Unawares of their lack of movement, Summer began to sprint, her eyes focused on the light. After reaching the rock, she peered carefully around the side of it. She was startled at what she saw and could not take her eyes off of the strange sight before her. Turning around to tell her friends of the fascinating sight, she discovered that she was alone. Walking back to the trail, she saw the five youth standing where she had left them. She yelled to them as loudly as she could.

"It's fantastic! I've never seen anything like this before! Come on Steve…Monica. Why didn't you follow me? Tykesha, Jose! It's okay!" Summer paused to see if they were coming.

The five youth huddled in a tight group, talking, as Summer became more and more impatient. She had been active in sports throughout Junior High School and had distinguished herself as "The Most Valuable Athlete" of the school, receiving first place in her boy/girl division in the one hundred-meter dash. In the yearbook, she was voted as the "Girl with the Most Energy". Anyone who really knew her said that she was the girl who was willing to try anything dangerous. It was this fact that worried her friends the most. After a moment, which seemed like an eternity to Summer, they slowly began the climb to the boulder where she stood. The sun had set and the light in the western sky was rapidly decreasing. The trail was barely visible. Although the group brought no flashlight, the brilliance of the light from behind the boulder provided ample lighting for the five youth to see around them for over fifty yards. Beyond was a foreboding wall of blackness that seemed to be teeming with the eyes of ravenous beasts of prey.

They found Summer shaking with excitement and anticipation. "It's beautiful. Take a look."

Summer led her friends around the boulder. Reluctantly, they followed close behind her.

The lightning and thunder had caused concern among the families of the hikers. "I'm worried that something has happened to them," said Mrs. Lopez, Maria's mother. The worry on the others' faces was evident. Even the smaller brothers and sisters sensed the potential danger that the teenagers might be in. "It's already eight-thirty," Mrs. Lopez stated.

3

Mrs. Solstice looked at her husband. Her expression communicated that they should not have allowed them to go.

"Did they have flashlights?" queried Mr. Solstice. None of the adults could remember if the group had taken any. Mr. Solstice continued.

"I think we should go look for them. Hank, Manual," he called to Steve's and Monica's fathers, "The three of us will go up the trail. Get your flashlights." The three men quickly assembled flashlights, first aid kits, ropes and other equipment that they thought could be used in an emergency and began walking up the trail.

It didn't take them long to reach the other side of the meadow. As they plunged into the deep forest, it became almost impossible to see without flashlights. They removed them from their packs, turned them on and continued.

Steve was the first to emerge from behind the boulder. He too gasped in wonderment at the scene before him. The reddish-blue color came from an oval-shaped light, about eight feet high and six feet wide. The light touched the ground. The base was flattened and about three feet wide. The shape of the light changed continually, writhing as if it were a living liquid or gas substance. The blue and red colors moved quickly around the oval in a random motion. Soon, all six teenagers were staring at the strange sight before them. Summer began to advance towards the oval light.

"Don't go near it!", exclaimed Maria with trepidation. …The girl that was willing to try anything dangerous, thought Maria over and over again.

Summer did not listen, but driven with curiosity, slowly neared the oval. She first walked around it. "It's flat on the sides of the light and on the other side the color is blue and green," she announced to her friends who now also were moving cautiously toward the light. As they reached Summer, they stopped and stared in horror as she put the tips of her fingers directly into the light, first on one side, then on the other.

"Hmmm... that's strange," Summer said as she returned to her friends. "When I put my fingers in the blue-green side it's cold and when I put them into the red-blue area it's warm. What do you suppose that means?"

Tykesha interrupted her. "I've seen you with that look before, girl, and I'm not liking it. Get some reason into that head of yours. Summer, let's get out of here!"

Her plea fell on deaf ears, as Summer returned to the oval light. "I'm going to stick my arm into the light on each side. Tell me if you can see it come through on the other end."

Jose, Monica and Tykesha closed their eyes. Steve and Maria stared in disbelief at Summer's complete lack of reasoning. They had seen this same behavior in school and almost every time it got her and sometimes them in trouble. First Summer reached into the light on the blue-green side.

"Your hand and arm came right through, Summer," Monica exclaimed nervously.

Summer carefully walked around to the other side and stuck her arm into the red-blue side. "Summer.... I....I don't see your arm or hand at all," Steve said, trying to stay calm. "Let's get out of here, now!... Why aren't you listening to us, Summer?"

"I'll come. I just want to try one more thing."

"I don't even want to know what you're going to do," Jose mumbled to himself softly.

Summer stood in front of the red-blue side and started walking toward it. When the front part of her body touched the light, she hesitated.

"This feels warm and nice", she said as if she were in a trance. She continued walking forward, disappearing into the oval light.

"Summer!" Tykesha yelled.

A scream came from within the oval light and Summer's hand appeared momentarily but disappeared as quickly as it had appeared. Then the fearful sound of her voice could be heard. "I can't get out of here without your help! Please help me! Oh no! There's something in here with me!" Another scream...... then silence.

Steve sprang into action and ran toward the oval light. As he approached, the light began to fade. He jumped into the air toward the red-blue side, but as he moved into the light, his whole body passed through. He fell onto the ground, scraping his elbows and tearing his jeans. The strange light had completely disappeared, leaving the youth in complete darkness.

It was now nine-thirty and still there was no sight of their children. The worry on the faces of the three men grew and they increased their pace. "At this rate, we should be nearing the part of the trail that will take us to the ridge in about twenty minutes," Hank said as they momentarily stopped to look at the map that they had brought with them. As they continued to walk up the trail they heard the faint sound of voices.

"Help! Who's down there with the lights? We need help!"

"That sounded like Steve's voice," exclaimed his father. The three began to run up the trail, breathing rapidly as they went. The final ascent leading to the ridge was reached and the men stopped to catch their breath.

"Steve, are you up there?"

"We're here Dad, hurry!"

The three men quickly reached their children. Steve ran and embraced his father. Monica and Tykesha sat, huddled by the boulder, sobbing uncontrollably. Jose sat by them, staring into the distance, unaware of the things going on around him. Jose's father had recently died in a car accident. The loss of Summer magnified his pain that he still felt. Maria was on her knees near where the oval light had appeared, feeling blindly in the darkness for any evidence of what might have happened to Summer. Manual and Hank rushed to help comfort the youth.

Mr. Solstice looked around for Summer, but could not see her. "Where's Summer?", he asked. Monica and Tykesha began to sob even louder than before.

Mr. Solstice became panicked. "Steve, what's happened to Summer!?"

"I'm sorry Mr. Solstice but we tried to stop her but she just jumped in and disappeared."

Mr. Solstice felt helpless. "What do you mean disappeared? Where's my daughter, Steve?" His voice grew louder.

Steve began from the moment that they had been awakened by the thunder and lightning until he had jumped through the oval light. By the time he had completed the account, all the youth had

6

stopped crying but they remained solemn and quiet.

"Steve, we have to try to find out more about this light that you saw." Turning to the other teens he continued. "I want all of you to try and remember everything that happened tonight."

"If we can find exactly what caused the appearance of the light, then what can be done?" asked Jose dejectedly.

"I don't know," confessed Mr. Solstice. "But we can't give up without trying. I have a friend who is an expert in science that I can call. Maybe he can give us some help. Let's get back down."

This is literally going to kill my wife, he thought. How am I ever going to tell her what happened?

As the group descended, he continued to rehearse over and over again how he would break the news to his wife. As they slowly entered the camp everyone ran through the darkness to meet the little group. The clouds had all but disappeared and a light breeze blew through the trees. The moon bathed the tops of the trees in its light.

Mrs. Solstice arrived first. She shined her flashlight at each of the weary hikers. Summer was not there. She looked at the sadness and pain in all of their faces.

"What happened?" she asked, looking at her husband for some hope. His face was filled with sadness.

"What happened to our daughter?" Mrs. Solstice demanded. She came close and they embraced. Both were in tears and said nothing for several minutes. The others gathered around them as they listened to what Mr Solstice would say. He couldn't recall what he had practiced as he walked down the mountain so he just told her the story related by Steve. Mrs. Solstice began to sob, overcome with grief. By the time that her husband had completed his story, the other mothers had congregated around her to comfort her.

"I can't believe that this has happened..." she said. "My daughter... where did she go?"

Manual interrupted. "We can't do anything until morning. We all need to get some sleep. In the morning, we can go up again. If there are any clues of what might have happened, they will be easier to find in daylight."

Reluctantly the group of friends separated to their own tents and retired for a long, restless night. Hunger had fled and sleep did not come easily. Throughout the night the sad hoot of owls seemed to express their feeling of remorse at the disappearance of Summer Solstice. By early morning, a deep sleep had overcome the exhausted campers.

The morning light was in the sky but the sun had not come over the tops of the mountains or the trees around them. Venus could be seen in the horizon. Dew bathed the flowers and plants exposed to the cooler morning air. Five-thirty in the morning was always beautiful. Mr. Solstice had habitually arisen early to view the wonders of the crisp, morning air, the melody of the birds and the first rays of the morning sun as they bathed the tips of the trees in its glory.

He quietly left his tent. No one stirred. He looked toward the trail through the meadow and, not seeing anyone up, decided to go up to the ridge by himself.

As he approached the large boulder on the ridge, he found himself praying, "Please God, let her be all right and help us find her." When he came from behind the boulder, he expected to see Summer running towards him to give him a hug. Only stillness and emptiness greeted him. Ahead, he could see the mountains covered with trees rolling on for at least twenty-five miles. Beyond the mountains, he could barely make out the outlines of Salt Lake City.

He turned around and viewed large mountains behind him, continuing for at least seventy miles. After that, the forms of the farthest mountains disappeared in the darkness of the early morning. To the south was a trail that followed the ridge in a downward slope. As he viewed the scene toward the north, the ten thousand-foot peak, Mt. Walamalee, loomed above him. Mr. Solstice returned to the huge granite boulder. He slowly approached the area that Steve had shown him the night before. It looked completely different. He squinted as the sun emerged above the eastern horizon.

Coming closer, he saw a definite black line on top of a rock at the exact spot where Steve had indicated that the red-blue light had rested. It looked like a mark that had resulted from the soot of a hot campfire. He looked closer at the ground on both sides of the rock. He recognized the shoe marks of his daughter. He shivered as he saw those marks go around the black line and then toward the black line on both sides. Finding nothing else, he decided to look at the area where the lightning had struck the ground.

He walked toward the area that Steve had pointed out. The unmistakable blackened remains of a tree were no more than fifty yards from the spot where the light had appeared. He walked quickly towards the peak and stopped by the old tree. Other trees like this one sparsely dotted the ridge. They were pine trees that had been stunted in their growth because of their altitude and position on the ridge. The trunk had been split in two and was charred black. The area around the tree also was covered with a burnt, black color. The smell of burnt wood permeated the air. Mr. Solstice was impressed by the similarity of this area to the black line he had just observed. He wished he had done better in science in school as he sought for a logical explanation. He looked all around the tree for additional clues and finding none, began to return to camp.

Arriving at the campsite, the younger children and adults were already up. Steve was just coming out of his tent and spotted Mr. Solstice in the meadow. He broke into a run until he reached Summer's father. "Did you find anything?", he said, breathlessly.

Mr. Solstice shook his head and described the things he had seen. Then he looked at Steve and said, "We need to break camp and get back to our homes. Ask the others to write down everything they remember about last night. I'll add my observations to your list and will call a friend of mine at Utah State University. Maybe he could give us some ideas."

Steve tried to interrupt, but Mr. Solstice continued, unawares of Steve's attempt to speak. "Our school library just got a new multi-media reference program about science. We should all meet there later today and look at that program. Maybe we can learn more about our observations while we're waiting for my friend to give us his opinion."

Steve decided not to say anything, so he and Mr. Solstice returned to the tents and instructed everyone to begin to break camp. An hour passed for the families to fold the tents, clean the camp and load the cars. No one spoke as they worked. They moved mechanically and without motivation.

The cars emerged from the mountain road onto the interstate highway. As they neared the mouth of the canyon, Mr. Solstice took out his cellular telephone and dialed the number of a long-time school friend of his who worked in the space program associated with Utah State University. After several rings, a familiar voice answered the telephone.

"Hello."

"Hey, Bill how are you doing?"

"Tom, is that you."

"In the flesh."

"It's good to hear your voice. You just about missed me. I was about to go to a meeting at the university."

"This won't take long, Bill. Summer has disappeared." There was silence on the other end of the line.

"Tom, that's horrible", Dr. Bill Winter finally said. "But why are you calling me. You should be going to the police."

"I know. But the way that she disappeared isn't a police matter."

"What do you mean, Tom?"

Tom Solstice briefly explained to his friend about the events of the prior evening. After finishing his explanation Bill asked, "Where did this occur?"

"On a ridge above Lambs Canyon. Why do you ask?"

Bill quickly offered an explanation in an unusually excited tone. "Two days ago an older couple were hiking on a ridge about two miles from where Summer disappeared. They reported seeing a light almost identical to the one you described to me. Our people didn't consider the report as valid. Your judgement I trust. I think this is something we'd better look at."

"Did you interview them in detail about their observation?" Mr. Solstice asked hopefully.

"No, our people didn't give any credence to their story."

"Did you get a telephone number?"

Embarrassed, Bill Winter hesitated, then responded, "I think someone took it but threw it away as soon as the couple hung up. Tom, I've got to get to the meeting now, but I'll call you later this evening and we'll begin to examine this in detail."

10

"Wait, Bill. Before you go. Do you remember where this couple lives?"

"If my memory serves me correctly, I think they live in Salt Lake City somewhere."

Tom Solstice thanked his friend and asked him to get back to him as soon as possible. After terminating the transmission he called information and obtained the number of the Salt Lake Tribune. He dialed the number that he was given, while his wife helped him steer the car. The voice of a young woman answered. Mr. Solstice quickly requested that a large announcement be put in tomorrow's paper on the obituary page.

"How would you like that to read sir?" the young woman asked.

"Will the couple who called the space program in Logan, Utah, reporting the appearance of an unusual light on a ridge in the Rocky Mountains outside Salt Lake City please contact Tom Solstice at 486-1989."

Mr. Solstice then obtained the number of the Deseret News, the other major Salt Lake City newspaper and made a similar request.

Terminating the second transmission, Tom Solstice finally became aware of his wife's strange looks and of his other children's gazes.

"What's the matter, Cheryl," he asked.

"I gathered from your side of the conversation that someone else has seen a similar light. But what I want to know is why you wanted to put the announcement on the obituary page?"

"The part of the conversation that you didn't hear was that the couple was older. I figured that most older couples would read the obituary page."

The family was silent the remaining twenty minutes to their home. The presence of only three children in their car was a painful reminder of the reality of the events that had occurred the night before. The last twenty minutes seemed like an eternity. After arriving and unpacking the car, Tom Solstice went into his study to write down all of the observations he had seen that day. In five other homes, Summer's friends were doing the same thing.

CHAPTER 2

The bold sound of the telephone filled Maria Lopez's home. "Yes?", said Maria's mother. "Hello, Steve. No. Maria isn't here. Yes. I'll tell her. She'll be excited about the news. Thanks for calling. Goodbye."

Not long after she had hung up the telephone, Maria walked through the door. "Hi Mom, any news from Steve yet?"

"He just called, Maria. Steve said to meet over at..." She paused and tears came to her eyes. Forcing herself not to cry, she continued. "...at Summer's house at six o'clock tonight. You're going to put together all of the information that you've written down."

A smile and a look of relief crossed Maria's face at the same time. All of Summer's friends had met at noon at the high school library on the day before and worked on the science program throughout the entire night. They returned to their homes by nine o'clock that morning. Maria had slept for only two hours when some of her friends had woken her up and had asked her to come to the mall to shop for school clothes. It required all of the self-control she had not to tell her friends about Summer's disappearance. She had successfully kept her promise to Mr. Solstice and now was excited about the prospects of the evening.

"Did Steve say whether Mr. Solstice's friend or the couple had called him yet?"

"His friend had given him information to help put your observations together, but had to go out of town yesterday after his meeting. He promised that he would call back tonight when he got home. The couple hasn't called yet." Mrs. Lopez turned to go back into the kitchen.

"Can we eat now Mom, please?" Maria pleaded with her mother. "I want to get over there a little early to look over some last minute things that I found in the library this morning."

"Now don't give me that look, Maria. I know it's important for you to go as soon as possible. I have dinner ready now. I was just going to put it on the table." Maria jumped towards her mother and

13

gave her a big hug and kiss. She literally catapulted herself from the room to clean up for the exciting evening ahead.

Six o'clock seemed like it would never come. Maria had already been at the Solstice home for more than thirty minutes when the others finally arrived. As they entered, the telephone began to ring. Cheryl Solstice answered it while Tom Solstice greeted Summer's friends.

"Dear, it's for you."

"Who is it?" Mr. Solstice asked as he came to the telephone.

"I don't know. It's a man and he wouldn't give his name."

Mr. Solstice picked up the telephone.

"Hello. Yes. Yes it is. Thank you for calling. The reason I put the ad in the newspaper is that my daughter and her friends have seen what appears to be the identical light that you have seen." The entire group of youth and Mrs. Solstice had now come close to the telephone, trying to understand what was being said.

"No", continued Mr. Solstice, "the people at the university thought that it was just a crank call, so they didn't keep your telephone number. When I told them our story, they wished that they had kept it." The voice on the other end of the line continued as Mr. Solstice listened carefully.

"Did it have a red-blue color on one side and a blue-green color on the other? Yes. Uh-huh. What happened just before the light appeared?" Again Mr. Solstice listened intently. Quickly, he took out his pen and began to write notes on a piece of scratch paper. He grabbed a second sheet and continued writing.

"May I have your telephone number so I can call you back?" He wrote down the number. "Thank you. You've been most helpful. You see, my daughter walked into the light she saw and disappeared. The information you've given me, plus that which we have, may help us understand what happened to her." He hung up the telephone and thought for a minute.

"Well, what did he want?" asked Tykesha. "What did he say?"

Mr. Solstice sat down on the barstool near the telephone. "The light he saw was identical to the one you have seen." Everyone exchanged excited glances. "It was a little earlier in the evening, but it was during a thunderstorm."

14

"Did lightning strike near them?" Cheryl Solstice inquired.

"They don't know. The forest they were in was very thick. They heard a loud clap of thunder, but they couldn't see how close the lightning was because of the thickness of the trees. By the time they came out of the forest and onto the ridge, the light was already there. They were too afraid to come close, but they did walk around it and described exactly what you kids saw."

Cheers of victory broke out around the kitchen. "So that means that it can happen again?" Steve asked hopefully.

"Well, let's go into my study and put our information together. We'll need to consider the factors that we think have the greatest possibility of causing the appearance of the light." They quickly walked into Mr. Solstice's study.

Six chairs had already been arranged around his desk. Steve looked at everyone. "Did you bring all of the research notes that you made, including the weather map?" They looked at each other, ashamed. "We forgot to do the weather map, Mr. Solstice", Tykesha confessed.

"That's okay. I think I have another one under all these papers here." They gathered around the map when it was found and noticed that a huge low pressure and cold front were over the Rocky Mountains on the day that Summer had disappeared. Then they began to combine their notes together and discuss the possible causes of the light's appearance.

It was now almost nine o'clock. Mrs. Solstice came in and looked at the group. The things they were studying absorbed everyone.

"That's got to be it!" Jose blurted out enthusiastically. He jumped up so quickly that he bumped the chin of Mrs. Solstice. She didn't even feel the pain because she was well aware that they had arrived at a possible explanation for the appearance of the red-blue, oval light. Tykesha was talking in loud, happy tones to Steve. Maria and Monica were crying for joy and hugging each other. The telephone rang. Mrs. Solstice was the only one who heard it over the noise of the excited group of youth.

"Hello. Yes Bill, thanks for calling. If I can get this group to quiet down, I'll let you talk to my husband." Mrs. Solstice walked

15

over to her husband and touched him on the shoulder. He looked at her as she pointed to the telephone. "It's Bill", she said loudly. He rushed to the telephone and took the receiver. The noise had quieted as the youth stopped to listen to the conversation.

"That's okay Bill. I'm glad that you got back to me. We think we understand the conditions for the appearance of the light. If the information you gave us is correct, we are now at the period of time for the light to appear again. By the way, the couple that saw the light called me just a few hours ago. They told me that there was a strong electrical charge in the atmosphere just before the light appeared. This is the same thing that happened to Summer and her friends." Tom Solstice stopped talking as he listened to a rather lengthy reply from Bill Winter.

"I don't understand Bill. Why do we have to do that?" Mr. Solstice paused as Bill Winter continued his explanation. "But that will take a lot longer before we can really find out what happened to Summer. Conditions are perfect right now during the maximum period of thunderstorm activity. If we wait for that, it may be too late."

Another long period of response came from the Utah State University space scientist. "I understand", sighed Mr. Solstice. "Thank you for calling."

Mrs. Solstice and Summer's friends waited for Mr. Solstice to explain the strange telephone call. Finally, with saddened eyes, he began. "I'm sure that you know who that was. He was happy that we figured out what caused the light, but he told us that we couldn't do anything about it until a special team from NASA and the United States Armed Forces arrived. They feel that it's too dangerous for us to get near the ridge. They plan to seal off the entire area when they get here and to set up a study team to examine the phenomenon."

"How long will it be before they get here?" asked Cheryl Solstice.

"Four or five days. We and the couple I talked to will be the only ones allowed to participate in that study." Tom Solstice's eyes became wet. "In four or five days the entire area will be sealed off and thunderstorm activity will probably be minimal for weeks to

16

come."

"That's ridiculous!" Steve spoke angrily. "We have to act now!"

"Steve! You can't… none of us can do anything. They feel that all of our lives will be in danger."

"But if we wait until they get here, and the light reappears, what are the chances that they will let us go into the light and try to find where Summer went? They won't even let us try it. You know that Mr. Solstice."

Mrs. Solstice interrupted. "Steve, we have already lost Summer. I can't bear the idea of losing you or any of Summer's friends. It's too risky. There's no guarantee that Summer is alive. Even if she were alive, there is no guarantee that you would find her. If you did, how could you get back?"

"With all due respect, Mr. Solstice," Jose responded, "Summer's last words were something like, I can't get back without your help. I believe she is okay and that we need to go after her. We need to do it now."

"No, I want everyone to wait until the study team arrives." Mr. Solstice looked into the eyes of each of Summer's friends. "Is that understood?"

They nodded sullenly in agreement. Maria's mother was called to pick up the group and return them to their homes. They thanked Tom and Cheryl Solstice and walked into the front yard of the Solstice home to await the arrival of the old, spacious van.

When they were out of hearing range from the house, Steve motioned for the others to come closer. "We can't wait. We have to go up now. Now is the maximum thunderstorm activity. We have to do something before the study team gets here."

"But how can we get to the ridge without Mr. Solstice and our own parents knowing where we're going?" Tykesha questioned. "None of us have drivers licenses." The others looked at Steve and waited for his answer.

"Doug Volcano is a Senior. I met him last week on the first day of summer football practice. He has his own car. I bet he would take us up if we paid his gas. We can tell our parents that Doug invited us to go on a trip to the zoo for the day."

17

"And if we find the light and go in and don't return, then what?" Maria asked.

"Then we won't be abandoning our friend. Our parents will understand that we have to do this."

Just then, Maria's mother drove up. The group agreed to Steve's plan, and Steve promised that he would contact Doug early the next morning.

The next morning, Steve called Doug Volcano. He had to tell him how Summer disappeared and why they needed to go immediately without their families knowing what they were doing. After hearing Steve's explanation, Doug readily agreed to take them up by noon that day. Steve then thanked him, pleading with him not to tell anyone about the plans.

Steve then called his four friends and told each to prepare a large pack of food and sodas and ask for permission to go to the zoo. All of Summer's friends did as Steve instructed. Each promised to return home by nine-thirty that evening, By twelve thirty, all were in Doug Volcano's car and were traveling on Interstate 80, leading towards the Lambs Canyon turnoff. They drove through the familiar groves of aspen trees. The bark of the trees was exceedingly white against the deep green background of small plants with delicate blue flowers. The trunks of the trees bent in the northwest breeze, as brilliantly-colored butterflies lazily rode the gentle breeze and bees went from flower to flower. After several miles of winding road, the aspen trees turned to stately, tall pines inter-spaced by an occasional aspen tree here and there. The floor cover changed from flowers to small shrubs, dead pine needles and fallen trees from the previous winter. The road increased in altitude as Doug's car followed its horseshoe and hairpin turns. The campground and meadow beyond were now in full view. Brilliant blue and yellow flowers covered the meadow. A slow-moving mountain stream meandered through the middle of the picturesque meadow. On the far side of the meadow, a lake built by beavers glimmered in the sunlight.

It had only been two days since they had been at the deserted campground. Doug looked into the rear-view mirror and spoke seriously. "Listen, if something happens to you, I could get into a lot of trouble. I really hope you know what you're doing. I'll go with

18

you but we have to leave here by eight tonight to get you back home in time. If it takes an hour to walk back here from the ridge, we will have to leave by seven."

Steve cringed inside. How can I leave at seven if the light hasn't appeared, he said to himself. He prayed that the light would appear before that time. Doug's car came to a stop.

The six young people got out of the car and moved quickly up the trail. White, billowy cumulus clouds were beginning to form in the sky above them as they left the meadow. By three o'clock in the afternoon, the group was standing by the boulder where the light had appeared.

"We aren't going to wait here all day, are we?," Tykesha asked impatiently. "Besides, there's nothing that we have learned that tells us that a thunderstorm, let alone a bolt of lightning, will hit at this one spot a second time."

"You're right, Tykesha," Jose said. "We'll have to move toward areas where we see the thunderclouds develop."

All six teenagers scanned the billowy white clouds around them. There were no cumulonimbus clouds anywhere in sight.

"This is just like the day we were here," Monica commented. "Maybe the thunderclouds won't develop until later. When they do, we have to be ready to move fast." After a moments pause, she continued. "I'm hungry. Let's relax here for a bit and eat something." Monica pointed towards the boulder where they had eaten their lunch two days before.

"And who's going to keep us awake after we eat?" Steve asked sarcastically. Everyone including Steve laughed mechanically at his comment. They sat down and ate but did not lie down for a rest. When they were done, they stood up and came from behind the boulder and looked around.

"I think I see a thundercloud beginning to form," Maria said, pointing toward the ten thousand foot peak. They all looked in dismay as the clouds began to form quickly around the mountain peak and to rise above the mountain.

"Oh no!" Tykesha groaned. "I don't want to climb to the top of that mountain. First of all, we'll be dead tired by the time we get up there and second of all, we could all be killed by lightning. Third of all...."

"Third of all, nothing, Tykesha." Steve stepped closer to her. "Look at me. We're here to try to find Summer. She would do the same if we had walked into that light and disappeared."

Tykesha began to cry. "I'm scared. I don't want to die now."

"I'm scared too," Steve said as he put his arm around her shoulder. He paused for a moment while Tykesha gained control of her emotions. "We're all afraid to die. But I'm not sure I could live with the knowledge that I didn't even try."

These words comforted all except Doug Volcano. The five friends began to walk up the ridge trail leading to the peak. Doug stayed behind and didn't move. Monica suddenly discovered that he wasn't with them. She turned around and saw him sitting on a small granite rock by the boulder. "Doug, aren't you coming with us?"

"No... no... I don't think so. I'm the driver, remember? I'll just sit here, and watch you. But remember, be back here by seven." Doug sat with his back against the larger boulder. He watched the group get smaller in size as they walked up the trail. They would disappear behind huge granite boulders and then reappear again as they continued the rugged climb towards the summit of the mountain. The clouds over the mountain darkened and grew rapidly in size. Soon, they covered the sun casting a shadow over the entire ridge. Doug had been concentrating so hard on the progress of the five youth that he didn't notice that similar clouds were developing above him. He jumped up, frightened, and looked around. He couldn't run anywhere that would not be under the ominous clouds. He yelled at the top of his lungs to the group in hopes to notify them that clouds were appearing everywhere.

Jose stopped. "Hold on. Did you hear someone yelling?" Everyone stopped and became very silent. "There... there it is again."

They turned toward the sound and saw Doug jumping up and down, waving his arms. "I wonder what he wants?" Steve said, scratching the back of his head. "Hello!", Steve yelled and waved his arms back at Doug. "What time do you have Ty.... Wait. Look, he seems to be pointing toward the sky....oh, my word... look at the clouds over Doug." Steve pointed at the rapidly growing cumulonimbus clouds. They looked above themselves and saw the same phenomenon. The wind was beginning to increase as it whipped strongly around their bodies.

"Lightning could strike anywhere from where we are to where Doug is and even beyond him". Jose gasped as he realized the almost impossible task of being able to locate the light in more than a mile of trail along the ridge. "Should we split up and wait at different places along the ridge?"

AI don't think it's a good idea", cautioned Steve. "If we split up too much, then maybe only one of us will get into the light if it appears. That might not be enough to help Summer return."

Lightning began to pass through the air and in between the clouds around them. Deafening thunder answered each lightning bolt. "I wonder if this was a good idea to come here?" Maria haltingly asked. No one answered. In fact, there was no time to answer, as multiple streaks of lightning flashed across the sky, sending the teenagers to safety behind a huge boulder. The wind increased in its ferocity and the loud thunder caused the youth to shake in fear. Dust blew into the eyes of the hiding group. Lightning struck the ground near Doug as he ran down the trail towards the forest. As the thunder resounded in their ears, Maria looked from behind the rock and saw him running down the eastern slope of the mountain back towards where he had parked the car. "Lightning must have hit near the rock where we ate. Doug's running like a scared rabbit."

"Has any light appeared?" Steve asked.

"No", answered Maria, peering at her watch. "In fact, the air isn't charged at all like it was the other night. But it's only four o'clock."

"Remember Maria," cautioned Tykesha, "the time wasn't a critical factor." Lightning struck again, this time on top of the peak. The flash of light and instant thunder surprised the youth and they swirled around.

"I feel it" Jose yelled over the deafening moaning and whistling of the wind. "The air is becoming charged." The others nodded as they felt the hair on their heads and necks begin to rise toward the sky. Another lightning bolt moved rapidly through the air, but this time, in between clouds. Although it was early, the density of the clouds, worse than they had ever seen, even two days ago, caused the surrounding area to be covered in darkness.

The group emerged from their hiding place, feeling frightened and disoriented, and began walking down the trail leading to the ridge. Lightning struck on the western slope of the ridge, not more than four hundred yards ahead of them. It was the largest bolt of lightning yet! The massive electron charge seemed to explode when it hit the ground. The hair on their heads received a strong, opposite charge and was more strongly attracted toward the sky. They froze as the thunder shook the ground. Doug was nowhere in sight. He had long since disappeared into the forest. Suddenly, the wind stopped. No birds or animals could be heard.

"Isn't this what happened the other night?" Steve looked concerned as he asked the question. His eyes turned from left to right. "Look! Is that a light against the trees over there?"

The group stared where Steve pointed. On the western slope of the ridge, towards the city, and beyond where the lightning had struck, there was a weak light reflecting against the trees.

"Quick!" Tykesha yelled. "We have to get there quickly!" She began running as fast as the terrain would permit. The others followed her. They were now within three hundred yards. The light illuminated the trees with greater brilliancy. Two-hundred yards. They weren't aware of the bruises on their feet as they stepped on sharp granite rocks covering the trail. Their thin-soled tennis shoes provided little protection. Leaving the trail, they headed toward the western slope of the ridge. Only one hundred and fifty yards now. The slope continued downward and the reflected light became brighter with every step. One hundred yards.

"Hurry!" cried Maria. "We have to get there before it disappears." Fifty yards. The direct light was now clearly in view. It was oval, only the color was blue and green.

"Maybe the blue-red color is on the other side of the light?" Steve said breathlessly as he read the thoughts of his friends. They now had arrived at the light. They stopped running but continued walking towards the opposite side of the oval light. As they came around to the other side, the familiar red-blue color could be seen.

"Quick, hold hands and let's go." Their hands were filled with sweat from nervousness, not knowing what to expect. One by one they disappeared into the light."

When the lightning and the wind had ceased, Doug took courage and ran back towards the ridge. As he arrived, he looked toward the peak. Not finding any of the youth, he began to look elsewhere. His eyes crossed to the western slope of the ridge. Instantly, his eyes were drawn toward a slender but tall oval light. What he saw was frightening. The images of five youth could be seen, holding hands as they were running toward the light. One at a time, they disappeared until they all had entered the light. Doug instinctively ran towards the light, but as he neared it, it began dimming and appeared to leave the ground. By the time he had run an additional hundred yards, the light had completely disappeared. Steve, Monica, Maria, Tykesha and Jose had vanished, without a trace. Complete silence. Frightening silence. He stopped and looked around and realized that he was all alone. He looked at his watch. It was only four-fifteen. The entire ordeal had taken only fifteen minutes.

The horror of his situation now fully hit him. He had to be the one who told the families what had happened and realized that serious consequences might follow. He knew that he couldn't bear the sorrow that would come to the lives of the five families. He turned around and began walking slowly down the trail that led to his parked car. Getting into his car, he drove slowly down the mountain road. Reaching the main highway, he turned toward Salt Lake City. It was the first time in his life that time had passed too fast. Before he knew it, it was seven thirty and he found himself standing in front of the door of the Solstice home. Mr. Solstice had been his favorite teacher during his first three years of high school. He shakily rang the doorbell and waited. He hoped that no one was home. The door opened and he groaned inside.

"Yes, who is it? Doug, it's great to see you. Please come in." Mrs. Solstice showed him in.

"I'm sorry to hear about Summer, Mrs. Solstice."

"Thank you Doug, but how did you hear?" She stopped and then looked behind him and a puzzled look crossed her face.

"Didn't you go with Summer's friends to the zoo this afternoon. Maria's mother told me you wouldn't be back until after nine tonight. Is everything okay?"

Before Doug had a chance to answer, Mr. Solstice had entered the room. "Hi, Doug," he said, greeting him warmly with a handshake. Doug's hands were moist and cold. "Doug, what's wrong? I don't believe I've ever seen you this upset before."

"Something terrible has happened." His words sent chills up the spine of both Tom and Cheryl Solstice. They brought him into the living room and he sat nervously on the edge of the couch. Mr. and Mrs. Solstice sat on either side of him. Their younger children ran into the room and were delighted to see him. They loved to watch him at each of the football games that their father had taken them to. They became silent as Doug began to relate his story to the Solstice family. As he concluded with the disappearance of the five teenagers into the light and the disappearance of the light itself, tears filled everyone's eyes. "I shouldn't have done it Mr. Solstice." He broke down, crying uncontrollably.

"Have you told the other families yet Doug?" Doug's face dropped and Tom Solstice realized that he had not told them yet.

"Well, before we go and tell them, I have to make a quick telephone call first." The relief in Doug's eyes communicated his gratefulness to Mr. Solstice's offer.

Mr. Solstice left the room and went to his study. He dialed the telephone. "Hello," Bill Winter answered.

"Bill, this is Tom. We have a problem."

"What's the matter, Tom?"

"Summer's friends conned one of my former students into driving them up to the ridge today. A violent thunder episode developed, the light appeared, and they all entered the light and disappeared."

Only silence could be heard on the other end of the line as Bill Winter tried to grasp the horrible tragedy that had just occurred. "I... I... this is bad!" He quickly organized his thoughts and continued. "I'll activate several local units of the guard and we'll go to the ridge tonight. I'll call Washington to see if the team can get here by tomorrow night. Can you and your former student meet us there?"

24

"Just as soon as we notify the families of Summer's friends."

"I don't envy your job, Tom. Good luck. It's close to eight o'clock now. We'll meet you at the Lambs Canyon turnoff at about midnight tonight. Oh, try to contact the couple that called us and get them to come with you, if you can."

"You bet, Bill. Thanks for your help." Tom hung up the telephone and looked for the notes where he had written the telephone number of the older couple, Vaughn and Mary Swanson. After a few rings, Mary Swanson answered. Tom explained the purpose of his call and requested that she and her husband join them.

"I'm not feeling well right now, especially to up to such a height. Let me go and see if my husband is able to go." Mary Swanson left to relay the telephone message to her husband. After a few moments, she returned to the telephone. "Hello, Mr. Solstice?"

"Yes, I'm still here."

"He said that if you would come and pick him up that he would gladly go. He doesn't like driving at night."

"I'll be happy to, Mrs. Swanson. Just give me directions to your home and I'll be by at about ten-thirty tonight." Mary Swanson thanked him and gave him instructions on how to get to their home.

Mr. Solstice then dialed the number of the Volcano home. When Doug's father answered, he identified himself and briefly reviewed the happenings of the day and his experience earlier in the week. He asked Mr. Volcano if Doug could accompany him to the ridge later that evening, assuring him that he would not be allowed to go near the light, if it appeared again, but would only be used as an information resource by the study team coming from Washington. Mr. Volcano gave his permission.

Tom returned to the front room. "Let's go Doug. After notifying the families, we'll stop by your house for your camping gear. We're going back to the ridge tonight." His wife looked at him, terrified for his safety. She wanted to keep him safely at home, but knew that this had to be done. Then he went into the garage and put his camping gear and the non-perishable foods that had not yet been put away from the outing into the car. Then, Doug and he began the most difficult task that they had ever done in their lives.

CHAPTER 3

Doug Volcano, Tom Solstice and Vaughn Swanson sat in silence as they neared the Lambs Canyon turnoff. Telling the families had turned out to be as bad as Doug and Mr. Solstice had imagined it would be. The loss of five more of their children was an almost unbearable burden for the six families. Tom had wished they could stay longer, but the families encouraged them to go, feeling that this was their only hope. Tom saw the Lambs Canyon turnoff sign and slowed his car. As he left the main highway, the headlights of his car revealed four military trucks and a private car. He pulled up to the small convoy and Doug, Vaughn and he got out of the car. Bill Winter ran to meet them.

"Bill, this is Doug Volcano and Vaughn Swanson. Doug and Vaughn, this is Doctor Bill Winter" They shook hands.

"Mr. Swanson, I'm sorry we didn't take your original call seriously. You can't imagine how many calls we get each month about different phenomena that people think they see."

"It's okay, Doctor Winter. My wife and I figured that our telephone call was ignored. I'm just sorry that the light has caused the disappearance of some fine young people."

"Bill, I'll lead you to the camp site. Were you able to contact the study team?"

"Yes. They're on the last flight tonight and will arrive at the Salt Lake International Airport at six o'clock tomorrow morning. My people will be meeting them and will bring them here. A special military unit is coming with them. About thirty men, I was told. Together with the twenty National Guardsmen that are here, we will have a small army."

"Good. Let's get going." The clouds that had covered the sky earlier were now completely gone. The stars were clear and bright. The small convoy continued up the small Lambs Canyon road. Once in the campground, the entire group began preparing their equipment for the long walk up to the ridge. Rifles, ammunition and other weapons that were unfamiliar to Mr. Solstice were part of the National Guard equipment.

Looking at the arsenal, Mr. Solstice said, "Bill, is all this firepower necessary?"

"Yes, Tom. Unfortunately, we don't know what or who we're dealing with and we have to be prepared for any situation."

When all the equipment was ready and packed securely, the group moved out into the meadow, with Tom Solstice at the lead. The air was still and dry. The journey was completed in record time. Tom was impressed at the rapidity with which the guardsmen moved with the heavy weight on their backs. The agility of Vaughn Swanson during the climb also was very surprising. He hoped that when he was his age he could still climb mountains the way he did. Finally, they arrived at the base of the final incline leading to the ridge.

The equipment was unloaded and tents set up in a clearing in the pine trees just below the ridge. Space was cleared for the additional thirty men that would arrive later that day. It was three-twenty in the morning as everyone lay down in their tents and quickly fell asleep.

By the time the morning sun was on the tents it was almost ten o'clock. Some of the men began to stir and emerge, stretching, while others slept on. Bill Winter was one of those who woke up as the sun hit his tent. Suddenly, the sun disappeared behind a large dark cloud. Bill turned to examine the cloud. It was a little early in the morning for thunderclouds to develop, however, the sky already was dotted with large cumulonimbus clouds.

"Everyone up!" Bill yelled. "We've got possible thundershower activity this morning." Within ten minutes the men were ready for the day.

"Let's look at what we have before we eat breakfast", Bill said authoritatively. He led the way up the remaining distance to the ridge. Doug and Mr. Swanson were near the front of the group with Mr. Solstice and Doctor Winter. As they reached the top of the ridge, they could see the sky more clearly. The cumulonimbus clouds were isolated and at least ten miles to the east. The clouds moved slowly toward the east and posed no immediate threat to the ridge.

"Let's get breakfast going", Doctor Winter told the commander of the National Guard unit. "I'm going to have these gentlemen show me where the oval lights were located."

Tom led the smaller group to the other side of the granite boulder and showed them the marks left by the first oval light. He pointed to the area where the lightning had struck the ground.

"Doug, are there similar marks where Summer's friends went into the light?"

"I don't know Doctor Winter," Doug responded. "I was so scared when I saw them disappear that I didn't even try to get close. I just wanted to go home. But I can show you about where it was." He led Doctor Winter, Mr. Solstice and Mr. Swanson down the western slopes of the ridge until they arrived at the area where he had seen the oval light.

"It was somewhere between the boulder over there and the burned area of the ground here where the lightning hit." Doug pointed at the two reference points.

The four split up and began searching every inch of ground. After almost thirty minutes, Doug called out, "I've found it"

The others came running. As they examined the mark, they saw that it was identical to the other mark where Summer had entered the light.

"Mr. Swanson, did you see a mark like this one when you and your wife saw the light?" Bill Winter waited patiently for his answer.

"The light never disappeared while we were there. We walked around the light, saw the same colors described by Mr. Solstice, but we left before it disappeared."

"Just how long did you stay to observe the light?" questioned Doctor Winter.

"Over a half an hour. It took us a long time to get up the courage to even get near the light."

"That's strange," mused Mr. Solstice. "In the two instances where people entered the light, it lasted about fifteen minutes. But in your case, it lasted longer than thirty minutes."

After examining the place where the lightning struck, the four returned to camp to eat breakfast. As they were eating, Doctor Winter received radio communication that the study team and special military unit were unloading their gear in the camping area. Several National Guardsmen were sent down the trail to help them with a special armored video probe for examining hostile environments.

It was close to two in the afternoon when they had arrived at the camp below the ridge. White cumulus clouds silently moved across the sky. A middle-aged woman and a gray-haired man, both in military uniform, came up to Bill Winter, and smiled dutifully at him. The woman identified herself first. "My name is Colonel Brenda Crater, head of the NASA Study Team for Unusual Sightings. It's nice to meet you in person."

"It's a pleasure," returned Winter as he shook her hand. "Have you received the update on the additional teenagers that entered the light?"

"Yes I have." Then looking at Tom Solstice she said, "Are you Mr. Solstice, the high school teacher?"

"Yes Ma'am, I am", he said and extended his hand to greet her.

"I'm so sorry about your daughter, Mr. Solstice...and about her friends."

"Thank you for coming Colonel. There are six families that have their hopes pinned on you to help our children." Colonel Crater's expression remained stern as she indicated that she and her team would do everything in their power to find the cause of the phenomenon and attempt to determine if there was any possibility of survival within the light.

The second officer stepped forward. "I'm Colonel Loess. I'm in charge of the special attack force assigned to the study team here." He extended his hand and the others greeted him warmly.

"Attack force?" questioned Tom Solstice.

"Remember, it's a precautionary move, Tom. We don't know what we're dealing with." Winter touched his friend on the shoulder as he spoke to him.

Colonel Crater looked at Doug and said, "Are you the young man who brought the five young people up here?"

"Yes I am," Doug looked down at his shoes as he answered very softly.

"Since you're the only one here when the last light appeared,

30

I'm going to be relying on you to give me a detailed description of all the things that happened before the light appeared. Could you come with us to the area where the five teenagers disappeared into the light?" Doug nodded and followed her and Colonel Loess and their men. Specialized sensing instruments were carried with them as they walked up to the ridge.

The group was gone for almost three hours. Occasionally Tom Solstice walked up to see what they were doing. Each time he saw them talking and using their sensing devices measuring the area around where the light had appeared. On his last trip up to the ridge he noticed that the wind had increased. Thunderclouds were beginning to form in the distance.

The group returned to the camp by five-thirty. Supper was prepared and eaten. An air of anticipation filled the camp. Six-thirty PM...no change in the weather.

The waiting had become unbearable for Tom Solstice. He stood at the top of the ridge looking in all directions. The sky was clearing and the evening star welcomed the night. Bill Winter walked up to the ridge and came to his side.

"The thunderstorms forecast for this afternoon and evening probably won't appear, Tom. They were only to be in isolated areas anyway. The forecast for tomorrow is for frequent thunderstorm activity. We'll probably have a better chance then." Reluctantly, Tom accompanied his life-long friend to the camp. Eight-thirty PM...clear...silence.

The pines bent against a gentle breeze. By the time that nine-thirty had come, the breeze had died and the stars glittered brightly in the sky. Tom Solstice resigned himself to wait for the next day. He went into his tent and lay down but could not fall asleep. The hours passed slowly. He didn't remember when he actually did go to sleep.

A loud clap of thunder sounded as if the lightning had struck right above them. It awakened the whole camp. The wind moved with gale force and an old pine tree toppled with a crash farther down the mountain. The sky glowed brightly once again and thunder sounded less than two seconds later. Tom rubbed his eyes and looked at his watch. It was only three in the morning. He could

31

hear an occasional drop of water falling onto his tent.

"It's time to get to work folks. It's promising to be a long day." The voice of Colonel Crater boomed loudly through the camp. National Guardsmen and the special units from Washington responded immediately. The wind increased in viciousness as it tore branches from the tops of the pine trees above them. Lightning continued to streak through the sky and the continuous crash of thunder resounded again and again.

"Be sure you have the land rover ready to go with the probe, in case we need it!" Her voice could now hardly be heard over the wailing of the wind and the creaking of the bending trees. Crater's men were scrambling out of their tents and preparing for action. The land rover and probe were carried to the top of the ridge and both the National Guard and the Special Attack Unit were running up the hill, weapons in hand.

Doug thought that the whole scene reminded him of a science fiction movie he had seen several months ago where an ugly monster had attacked a small community in the United States. His thoughts were interrupted by Colonel Crater's voice.

"Doug, come with me. I want you to tell me when the conditions are the same as the other day." Doug quickly followed her as she literally ran up the trail to the large boulder. He had a hard time keeping up with her.

As they reached the ridge, the scene before them caused them to stop. Multiple fingers of lightning flashed across the sky. One bolt hit the top of a mountain about two miles away. A tree split in two and millions of tiny sparks exploded in all directions. The lightning increased but it still was centered close to the mountains two miles away. The thunder was deafening. While the group was staring intently into the distance, lightning commenced just over the ten thousand-foot peak to their left. The thunder shook the ground under their feet.

"Colonel Crater!" Doug yelled. "We're getting close. If we start feeling the hair on our necks stand up, the light might appear somewhere on this mountain!"

The lightning increased over the peak. Suddenly streaks of lightning shot through the air directly overhead. Its intensity increased until the entire air became strongly charged. There was hardly more than a tenth of a second in between the enormous claps of thunder that incessantly smashed against the ears of the awestruck onlookers. A massive bolt of lightning came from a cloud above them and struck a small tree on the eastern slope of the ridge, burning it to a crisp. The thunder that followed sounded like the explosion of a large bomb. The explosion shook the ground and the bodies of those who watched. Suddenly, the wind stopped. The silence was filled with fear of the unknown.

"These are the exact conditions," Doug said breathlessly.

"Keep an eye out for a red-blue, oval-shaped light!" Colonel Crater cried to her men.

A red-green light began to appear about a tenth of a mile beyond where the lightning had hit the tree. It began to glow brighter and brighter.

"Let's move!" came Colonel Crater's command. The entire group of men began to run as quickly as they could. As they neared the light they decreased their pace to a cautious walk. The military readied their weapons. The light was extremely bright; blue-red on one side and blue-green on the other. They brought the sensing equipment near the light and recorded the physical conditions, energy and qualities of the light. Two video cameras recorded all of the events.

"Colonel Crater. There is an extremely high-energy field associated with the red-blue side of this light!"

"Get the land rover and probe ready and make sure the video camera is operational. We're going to send it into the red-blue side first." The light grew in intensity. To Doug, it appeared to be twice as big as the one the five teenagers walked into.

The weapons were readied. The electricity of the land rover was turned on, the correct functioning of the probe and video equipment verified and the land rover slowly began to move toward the blue-red light. Everyone was shocked when the rover's nose entered the thin light but did not appear on the other side. It proceeded into the light until it had completely disappeared. The technicians of the probe viewed the video screen, each scene being recorded. All of Crater's team congregated around the monitors.

"My word!" Crater exclaimed. "It looks like the control center of a space craft. The monitor showed colored lights of panels that were blinking on and off and two or three monitors with some kind of data crossing the screen.

"There doesn't seem to be anyone in the room, Colonel."

"Can we get the rover into any other part of this craft?" Crater asked.

"We can't see any other entrance or exit except for the light behind the rover. Wait... what's that. Oh no, God help us!" A solid portion of the wall of the control room melted away and the most hideous creature they had ever seen emerged from its opening. It had two arms and feet, but was completely covered with hair and a green-colored liquid slime. The three eyes of the creature caught sight of the rover and opened its mouth, showing long, sharp teeth. It appeared to be screaming.

"Quick, reverse the rover!"

The rover began to move in reverse toward the light. The monitor showed that the creature had begun to pursue the machine. "The rear of the rover is coming out of the light!" one of the study team members yelled, excitedly. As half of the land rover appeared, it suddenly stopped. The wheels continued to move, but it was as if the rover was stuck somewhere. It slowly was pulled back into the light. As it disappeared, all of the monitor screens blanked out. They now had no control over the rover at all.

The light began to diminish in intensity and then, finally disappeared. "I think we have a serious problem," Colonel Crater said in a low tone. She instructed her communications specialist to contact the Washington office with the news. Tom Solstice watched with a feeling of terror and hopelessness.

CHAPTER 4

The five teenagers wanted to close their eyes as they neared the red-blue side of the light but forced them to stay open. Their hearts pounded as they came to within five short paces of entering the light. So deep was their commitment to their friend that they didn't hesitate when the thought hit each of them, almost simultaneously, that they might never see their friends and family again.

The forceful, cool, gusty wind completely vanished as they entered the light. Warmth and calm covered them like a down-filled blanket on a chilly winter night. They recalled what Summer had said about the feeling of warmth when she had placed her hand into the red-blue side of the light. The five began to walk more slowly. The red-blue colors continued to move in random directions in front of them, causing them to feel dizzy. It reminded them of the fun house of an amusement park.

"Look," Steve whispered to the others, "the lights are beginning to disappear in front of us." All five paused, and stared at the lights fading out, one by one. Tykesha glanced behind them. The moving red and blue colors behind them were increasing in intensity.

She and her friends looked back at the disappearing colors again. What they saw caused them to gasp in amazement. The blue and red colors from the light reflected on a smooth, metallic floor in front of them. Dials and lights of different colors blinked on and off on the walls around the room. On the far wall, a television monitor displayed the mountains where they had been standing, only moments earlier. In the distance, they could see the occasional flashing of lightning bolts as they shot down from the thick, black clouds. To the right of where they stood was an even stranger sight. The trunk of a single, small pine tree disappeared into the metal-like floor. The tree above the floor was motionless, as if it had been startled by their sudden appearance.

"Is this a space ship or something?" Jose mumbled quietly.

"If it is," responded Maria softly, "that tree is the pilot. Do you think it talks?"

"Don't be silly." Steve continued in a whisper. "That's just a tree." Suddenly the tree began to move, as if a light summer breeze had been blowing, yet the air in the room where they stood was motionless.

The reflection of the blue and red lights on the floor began to fade. They turned around in time to see the last of the lights disappear behind them. A metallic-like wall appeared where there once were lights.

They looked again at the pine tree. As they watched the tree move, a yellow light above the tree began to increase in intensity. Then, periodically, it began to change to a white light and then back to yellow in the same rhythm as the movement of the tree. The teenagers were frozen with fear. They watched carefully as the tree continued to bend. Everyone but Monica was so intent on watching the tree that they were not aware that the red and blue television monitors to the left of the wall in front of them were slowly disappearing.

Monica had been silent the entire time. Suddenly, she blurted out in a loud, nervous voice. "The m…m…monitors o…on the left just disappeared and a d…door just appeared in the s…s…same spot." They waited cautiously, unable to move. Their minds raced with visions of all of the worst possible creatures that they had seen in horror movies. After all, Summer had said that something was in there with her.

Suddenly, before their eyes, something began to pass through the metallic door, without it opening. Its features, at a distance, were grotesque. Once it was in full view, it advanced slowly towards them. With each advance they stepped back, until they were trapped against the metallic wall behind them. Now that it was very close, they could clearly see its features. The creature had two arms and webbed hands, three eyes and a green slime that covered its entire body. Large pieces of hair also covered most of its body but the constant wiggling motion made the hairs appear like large worms. At first the teenagers thought that they saw feet, but soon recognized that what they thought were feet were only extensions of the green substance, on which it slid across the floor. The creature's mouth was large and full of sharp teeth, the points of which were bathed in blood.

When the youth saw the blood, they gave up hope and thought that they were already too late to save Summer. They now were sure that they would be the next meal for this "thing". Summer's friends were shaking with apprehension as the huge creature towered above them. It stood still and glared menacingly at them and they hardly could look back.

Tykesha finally gathered courage and spoke loudly. "What have you done with our friend, Summer?" There was no response. Tykesha spoke again. "Do you speak English or are you deaf? We've come to help our friend, Summer Solstice. Where is she?"

To their surprise, the creature again did not respond, but a physical change began to take place. Tykesha and her friends held their breath. Little by little, parts of the creature began to disappear. Finally, the transformation was complete. The little group stayed together as they slowly came closer to see the results of this unusual transformation. Floating in the air above them was a strange looking man with no hands, arms, legs or feet. His hair was long and gray and his eyebrows and mustache bushy and green. He looked gentle yet the red in the pupils of his eyes caused the youth to hesitate. He noticed this and spoke to them in a low tone.

"My name is Eclipse. I want to welcome you to my transporter. Summer told me that you would come. I had hoped that she was right. I am grateful that your friendship has brought you here. My entire planet will be grateful to what Summer and you will do for me."

Steve looked puzzled. "Planet?" he said. "What we will do for you? I want to know what you've done with our friend? How do we know that you're telling the truth?"

Eclipse looked at the monitor on the wall and the scene changed from the outside of the Interstellar Transporter to another part of the huge, but invisible spacecraft. Summer was sitting at a computer and studying some diagrams that were on the screen of the computer. When her friends saw her they cheered. Summer looked up from her work and towards another monitor.

She jumped up as she recognized her friends. "You came! Oh, thank you for coming. For a while I thought that you might not be able to!"

"All right, girl!" Tykesha blurted with joy and frustration. "What's going on here?"

Summer quickly responded, her voice filled with concern and enthusiasm. "Eclipse's home planet is dying and he asked me to help him. But what he needs is too much for just the two of us."

"Home planet dying? Wait a minute Summer, what have you gotten us into now?" Steve frowned as he spoke.

Eclipse interrupted. "Your friend, Summer, has agreed to travel with me to a planet in a galaxy far away from here. It is similar to both my planet and to yours. My people, over a period of many years, did not take care of the planet and so, the plant and animal life are dying."

"Wait a minute," Steve interrupted. "Why do we have to use that other planet when all you'd have to do is take things from our planet to save yours?"

"Because the same thing is happening to your planet. I cannot deplete a planet of its resources when they are already too low."

"Come on," Summer said in her usual impatient manner. "He really needs our help! We have to obtain the things that will give his planet the ability to survive!"

Steve looked at the others in a questioning manner. Summer waited for their response. "What do you think?" he said. Eclipse looked on quietly as the five youth contemplated Steve's question.

"Let's do it! We'll be the only teenagers in the whole world who've ever been outside earth before. Besides, going to the Mall to shop for school clothes and the first day of our freshman year would be boring compared to what's about to happen to us." Monica looked determined as she made the statement.

"That's if we really will come back to earth," Jose muttered doubtfully. "And what good is this journey. No one will believe our story anyway." The five youth looked at Eclipse.

"I have safely traveled through space for hundreds of years. There are many dangers, but I will help you get the knowledge and the training that you will need to survive. As long as you learn well, you will return unharmed."

Eclipse stopped talking to wait for their response. The five teenagers looked at each other and after a short moment, nodded their heads in agreement.

"Okay, Eclipse, take us to Summer. We'll help you all that we can." Steve almost smiled as he spoke. The adventure in front of them had caused him to be filled with a cautious, excited anticipation.

"You will be greatly rewarded for what you will do. Thank you my friends."

The group followed Eclipse as he floated through the metallic door. "Wait a minute Eclipse," Steve called just as he was disappearing through the metal. "We can't walk through a solid piece of metal like you can."

Eclipse re-entered and looked at Summer's friends. "Just try and you will see." He turned around and floated back through the door and disappeared from their view. The little group stared incredulously at each other.

"Well, if we can walk through a light into a space ship, then we can walk through a solid door," Jose declared with a guarded confidence. He began to walk toward the door. Just before his body came into contact with the metal, he stretched out his arms and hands to prevent injury when he hit the solid metal. To his surprise, his arms and hands disappeared into the metal. He continued and walked through the metallic door. The others stood in wonderment as he too disappeared. After only a short wait, the others walked quickly through the metallic door beginning an experience that would change their lives forever.

As they walked through empty corridors, Maria looked curiously at everything. Finally, she couldn't stand not knowing the answers to the questions that were coming to her mind. "Eclipse," she said. "How can a light be a door into your space ship?"

"When my transporter is visible, a regular door will allow you to enter and leave. When it is invisible, any electric field generated by a strong source of electromagnetic disturbance can cause a connection to occur between the visible world and the invisible Interstellar Transporter. If you pass through the light, it is like entering a door into the spacecraft. Since there is only one way in, you can only enter one way through the light. When this door is open, when I am invisible, I cannot leave a planet until the door disappears."

Maria asked her next question. "You said something about a galaxy. What is that? How far are we going to travel and how long will it take us? When will we get back?"

Eclipse hesitated a moment, then turned and looked at Maria. "A galaxy is only a small part of our universe. There are billions of galaxies in the universe. Each galaxy is made of billions of suns and planets. The suns hold the planets together. The sun and planet systems are held together by strong forces of a large center of each galaxy. We will be traveling to the far ends of the universe and if we are able to collect the material I need within two or three days, our total journey should take only a week or two at the most, as measured by your earth time."

They continued walking for almost five minutes. Finally they entered the room where Summer was working. She jumped up and ran to them and embraced each of her friends. They cried because of the safety of their daring, but special friend.

After several minutes of sharing experiences from the time of Summer's disappearance, Eclipse interrupted. "It is time for us to go. The electrical disturbance has momentarily passed which will allow us to leave your planet. Everyone, please sit down in a chair around this computer."

They all complied with his request. They watched as he floated toward a wall that looked like a clear crystalline-like rock. He looked at the "rock" and concentrated. Suddenly the entire crystal was filled with a three-dimensional picture of the mountains around them and the sky above them. Eclipse began to speak in a language that they could not understand. In response to what he said, dials and lights around the crystalline screen began to flash on and off. A humming that sounded like the engine of a quiet, powerful truck began to cause a slight vibration in the floor of the transporter. Eclipse continued a series of commands in the strange language and each time he spoke, additional lights could be seen and sounds heard. "Prepare to leave the planet," he said as he glanced at the youth.

A buzzing sound began, at first silently and then with increasing intensity. Eclipse frowned and glanced at a series of symbols that appeared on a small screen. "This is not good," he mumbled to himself.

"What's the matter, Eclipse?" Summer waited for his answer but he was deep in thought. "Is there something we can do to help?" Summer again awaited his reply.

After several minutes of silence, Eclipse began to speak. "The main thrusters that will allow us to go beyond the speed of light were damaged in the last large lightning discharge that occurred before you entered the light." After another long pause, he continued. "If we leave now without repair, it will take us over a million of your earth years to get to our destination"

"How long will it take to repair?" Summer asked.

"About thirty-six earth hours. You will have to forgive me. I have waited so many years to find someone to help me that I have grown very impatient."

"Why can't you do this by yourself, Eclipse?"

Eclipse turned toward Tykesha. "All of my people have hands, arms, feet and legs like you do. Many years ago, I became ill with a rare disease which made it necessary for them to be cut off. Since then, I have developed my mental powers to do many things, but that which must be done on the planet we will travel to, needs hands, arms, feet and legs."

"Why won't any of your people help you?"

"They do not believe that our planet is in danger of dying, Tykesha. I left almost four earth years ago in search of someone to help me. Just recently, I have heard reports of drastic changes in the climate, disappearance of whole species of animals and plants and a decrease in the amount of good air for us to breath. My people are now just beginning to realize that our planet is in danger. By the time they will want to help me, it will be too late to obtain what we need to save our planet."

There was a stillness that came over the entire room as the little group of friends contemplated how hopeless his situation seemed. Eclipse turned to begin the repairs. As he left he called back to the youth, "There are resting quarters off of this room. Please go and get some sleep. Our journey will be very tiring and you will need to be alert as we begin your training when we leave your planet."

Once he left, the youth stared at the beautiful mountain scenery on the crystalline screen. It's three-dimensional qualities made it appear like they were actually outside. The sun was beginning to disappear in the western horizon. "I can't believe how real this looks," said Maria in a sad voice. She already was missing the world they were about to leave. "I feel like I could touch that rock over there. This is weird."

"I'm sleepy," Steve said. "We haven't slept well since you disappeared, Summer." He looked again at Summer to assure himself that she was really there. "Summer, how do we know that you are really you and not some television screen or robot?"

Summer giggled and got up and touched him on the shoulder. "Go over there and see if you can touch that rock over there. You won't feel it at all. I know because I tried to touch my dad when he came up alone to the ridge here on the morning after I entered the light. But you can feel my hand when I touched your shoulder." Summer turned and walked toward one of the rooms and called to Tykesha, Monica and Maria. "This is the girls sleeping quarters. That one over there is for the boys." One by one, the youth got up and entered their sleeping areas and quickly fell asleep.

The crystalline screen was still on when Summer and Maria walked into the control center of the interstellar transporter. "It's already after ten o'clock," Maria said, surprised that they had slept so long. The two girls looked at the large cumulonimbus clouds in the sky. Suddenly a movement at the top part of the ridge caught their eye. In the distance, they could see four figures approaching the invisible ship.

"I wonder who that could be?" mused Summer. After a few moments, she gasped. "It's my dad and his friend, Dr. Winter! But who are those other two people with him?"

Maria looked closely. "I don't know who the older man is, but this other one is Doug Volcano."

"Who's he and what's he got to do with us, Maria?"

"Well, your dad wouldn't drive us back up after one of his friends at NASA told him not to. We couldn't leave you stranded, so we convinced Doug to drive us up and wait for us, in case the light didn't appear. I guess Doug went back and told your dad that

42

we had disappeared into the light."

"His friend at NASA is Dr. Winter. He's a space scientist. I wonder if that's him," she said pointing to a third person. By this time the other four youth had gotten up and had come to see what Summer and Maria were looking at. Summer became extremely agitated.

"Somehow, I <u>have</u> to communicate with my dad to let him know that we're okay. But Eclipse just isn't around when you need him." She looked at the control panel and pushed the first light that her hand could reach. Nothing happened. Frustrated she yelled, "Eclipse, where are you?"

At that moment Eclipse floated through the door. "Eclipse, how can I contact my dad to let him know that we're okay? Look at the worry on his face." She pointed to her father. The group watched the four as they searched the area.

"I'm sorry Summer. The only way that he can hear you is if you leave the transporter. Only mechanical things can exit back into the visible world from the invisible transporter. That which is living would be destroyed. That's why I pulled you back in when you first tried to leave. The only way that you can leave the transporter is for me to inactivate the invisibility device. There are a large number of armed military men on the other side of the ridge and another group is on its way up the trail to the ridge. They are all heavily armed with powerful weapons that would permanently damage my ship. My defense mechanisms are not working either. If my ship were to appear, none of them would wait to understand what is going on and would attack me and take you back to your homes. I could not complete my mission and my family would die."

Summer's head bowed and tears came to her eyes. A feeling of despair swelled within her. Tykesha rushed to her side, putting her arms around her shoulder. Fighting back the tears, Summer rubbed her eyes and looked up at the alien. "I understand Eclipse."

The group watched as Summer's father, Doug Volcano, Dr. Winter and the other man searched the area. Steve interrupted the silence. "I'm hungry. Do you eat food, Eclipse? I sure hope so, because, if we're gone long, I'm going to die of starvation."

Eclipse smiled. "Of course, I do. My diet is much the same as

43

yours with one exception. We do not have what Summer described to me as fast food businesses. We also have no prepared cereals." He led them to the dining area from which they sampled what tasted, but did not look like, eggs and bacon. There was a liquid that tasted like orange juice but had a purple color. The youth chose not to ask him exactly what they were eating and drinking but were grateful that, at least, the taste was similar to what they knew on earth.

After eating a large meal, Eclipse returned to the repairs of the thrusters and the defense mechanisms of the transporter. Summer took her friends back to the main control room of the ship and began to show them what she had been learning on the computer about electricity, light and the weather and climate of the earth. They also discovered a variety of strange "inter-galactic" computer games with three-dimensional figures. They became engrossed with solving the games as it took them through different star systems.

"I thought that young earth life forms got hungry more often than this!" Eclipse said in a booming voice. The startled group of teenagers jumped. They looked up from their computer game at the crystalline screen. The light of the stars shone brightly in the clear, black sky. They were shocked that they hadn't even noticed the setting of the sun.

Maria looked at her watch. "It's almost nine thirty. I can't believe how fast the time passed. These computer games are sure fun, Eclipse."

Ignoring her comment, Eclipse continued. "The thrusters and defense mechanisms are repaired. Within four hours, there will be sufficient energy transferred to their power systems to allow us to leave your planet. Quickly, go and get something to eat and then rest. We will begin your training after we leave your planet."

The youth quickly responded. There were no arguments because they now felt the extreme hunger that had been hidden by their fascination with the computer games they had played for over eleven hours. They returned to their sleeping quarters and went to sleep.

The sound of thunder startled Summer and her friends. They quickly got up and went to the control room. Eclipse was already

44

there. The expression of worry was clearly visible in his face.

"What's the matter?" Summer asked softly.

"Conditions are fast approaching which will allow the opening of the door of the ship once again. We won't have time to leave before that happens." The sky was illuminated by multiple arms of lightning once again and thunder quickly followed each burst of light. The invisible transporter was not affected by the sound waves of the thunder like the ground was.

"Look!" Steve yelled in surprise. "A whole army is approaching us! Are we visible, Eclipse?"

"No, Steve. But their intention is to explore the light when it appears." Another flash of lightning illuminated the military force that was fast approaching them.

Eclipse continued. "See that object they are carrying?"

Steve and his friends nodded their heads. "I believe that is a mechanical probe of some sort. That is what they will send into the light."

A large lightning bolt struck the ground and thunder followed.

"The door is open. I must go and destroy the probe when it enters the transporter."

Eclipse floated toward the door of the control room. Summer and her friends watched as he transformed himself back into the monster. Suddenly, the image of the crystalline viewer changed and they recognized the room of the ship where they had entered. The little pine tree was very still. They watched and waited in suspense as they viewed the empty room.

The probe slowly entered the room from the left of the crystalline screen. The red-blue light reflected strongly from the floor. It seemed like the probe was moving in slow motion. It passed behind the pine tree and then moved to the middle of the room and stopped. Its television camera was moving from side to side scanning the contents of the room. The metallic door, at the right of the room, began to appear.

Within seconds of the appearance of the door, Eclipse appeared as he floated through the door, disguised as the horrible monster. He moved steadily toward the probe. As he approached, the probe began to reverse its direction rapidly. It reached the opening of the light and was beginning to exit into the visible world. Before it completely left, the monster's arm quickly moved forward and, to the amazement of the spellbound youth grew and extended by at least five-fold. The exiting probe halted its movement and an unseen power caused it to shake and begin to return into the interstellar transporter. As it reached the huge web-like "hand" of the monster, the entire probe vaporized.   Seconds after that, the light disappeared. Eclipse turned and began to float back to the control room.

Summer and her friends could not believe what they had seen. They were still staring at the empty room where the probe had disappeared when Eclipse came through the closed door. Startled, they looked up. He had transformed himself back to his regular appearance.

"Within fifteen minutes, the conditions will be perfect for us to leave. Please sit down and I will begin the launch sequence once again."

After taking their seats, Summer and her friends watched as Eclipse followed the same procedures that he had done previously. This time no buzzer sounded and they saw the earth begin to recede as the interstellar transporter slowly lifted off of the ground. The darkness of the night made it almost impossible to see anything in the crystalline screen except for the lights of Salt Lake City.

"Look!" said Jose. "You can see the lights of Salt Lake! I never realized they were so cool." The little group of friends stared longingly at the lights that they knew as home. Suddenly, the lights disappeared. Jose looked curiously at Eclipse.

Understanding his confusion, Eclipse answered his unspoken question. "Jose, we have passed through the clouds and they are hiding the lights of your city. Soon you will see the lights of your entire country."

The youth stared intensely at the screen. Not long after Eclipse had answered Jose, each of the six youth gazed at the sight before them. In the darkness they saw the outline of the entire United States with lights that came from cities all over the country. The east and west coasts were the most easily seen because of the density of the lights of the crowded metropolitan areas.

"I don't believe I've seen anything so beautiful before." Summer could not take her eyes off of the screen. As the transporter went higher into the atmosphere, the outline of the United States became smaller. It wasn't long before they could see almost the entire Northern Hemisphere of Earth. The light from the rising sun bathed the Atlantic Ocean, the eastern parts of the South America and all of Europe and Africa. The entire United States and most of South America as well as the Pacific Ocean were still cloaked in darkness. Clouds covered large areas of the Atlantic Ocean. They saw the earth rotating toward the sun in the east, uncovering more and more of the eastern seaboard of the United States.

"It must be early morning on the East Coast," Steve said reverently. The earth now began to get smaller and they could see the entire planet all at once.

"Oh, look!" Tykesha said breathlessly. "The earth has the shape of the gibbous phase of the moon that we learned about at the high school library." The greater part of the right side of the blue planet they called home was brightly illuminated. The left side, where they had left moments before, was covered with the darkness of the earth's shadow. "It's hard to believe that I'm here and watching all this." Without saying anything, the others all nodded.

The interstellar transporter stopped when it was two hundred thousand miles from the Earth. "Why are we stopping, Eclipse?" Jose asked meekly. "Did we run out of gas?"

Eclipse smiled. "We have stopped to prepare the transporter for super-light travel. We must begin your training while we travel. All your lessons have been programmed into this computer. It is essential that you learn them well. If you do not, my planet will die and we may die as well. The youth seriously considered the gravity of the situation that they were in.

Eclipse continued speaking. "You will first learn about the birth of our universe and of planets in general. The things you will learn are similar throughout the entire universe, including on your planet. You will learn why we are able to travel in space and on planets. You must learn about where the energy for planets come from, how planets change and the things needed for life to survive on a planet.

You will learn about the different areas where living things exist together with other living and non-living things and how weather and climate control the kinds of life that live there. These areas are called ecosystems. Some call them biomes."

"How long do we have for the study, Eclipse?" Summer asked.

"That all depends on the velocity that we will be going, Summer. We will be traveling at one tenth the speed of light at first and when we leave your solar system, we will travel at a velocity that is much greater than the speed of light. Once we leave your galaxy, we will be traveling even faster than that."

Eclipse returned to the control center of the spacecraft. He spoke a command and the earth quickly shrunk to a small dot. Summer and her friends sat down around the computer and turned on the program that Eclipse had made for them. The images appeared on the monitor and they began their training.

Concentration was almost impossible. The other planets of the solar system were rapidly appearing and then shrinking in size and the youth were captivated as they saw them up close for themselves. Soon, only the sun was visible and it continued to get smaller also.

"Look at our sun ", said Tykesha excitedly. "It looks like the stars we see from earth! I never knew that if we got far enough away from Earth that our sun would look like a star."

"That is because each of those stars is a sun," explained Eclipse while the youth looked on in amazement.

"Why are all the stars grouped together in a narrow band like that?" questioned Summer.

"You are seeing the edge of your galaxy. It is only ten light years thick." Eclipse paused for a moment and watched the fascination on the faces of his six new friends.

"Look how far we've traveled", Steve said, shaking his head in disbelief.

The speed of the interstellar transporter was constant. The view on the crystalline screen was quickly changing. It was not long before the entire Milky Way Galaxy could be seen at once. After several moments, Summer began speaking very softly. "If I weren't seeing the Milky Way galaxy with my own eyes I would say that I was dreaming. I've already pinched myself once and I didn't wake up in my bed at home." The others could identify with her feelings. Summer continued. "I never knew how small the earth was in comparison to the whole Milky Way galaxy."

As the galaxy slowly became smaller in size the entire view on the crystalline screen became dark except for the stars that filled the universe in all directions. Finally, the galaxy became so small it looked like a single brilliant star. Many other brilliant stars could now be seen, each representing a separate galaxy.

Suddenly, the view on the screen began changing more rapidly. "How fast are we going, Eclipse?" Jose said.

"We have accelerated to thirty billion times the speed of light." No one said anything. How could such a thing be?

"What are you doing, Steve?" Summer said, as she noticed him touching his hands and face.

"I once read a science fiction novel about people traveling beyond the speed of light. I remember that it described that their features physically changed and that they were distorted and looked gross. I was just checking." Steve looked normal to them. Laughter exploded in the control room. It felt good to laugh once again.

Monica had just finished working out some calculations on a piece of paper. She looked up at her friends with a big smile on her face. "I just figured out that at this rate of travel we will be at our destination in about six months."

"Six months!" complained Tykesha. "We're going to completely miss our freshman year of school!"

Summer smiled. "Just look around, Tykesha. We'll be learning more than we ever could if we took classes." Tykesha stopped for a moment and thought. She smiled as she saw Summer's point of view.

Jose looked frustrated. "You know, I wouldn't like living out here where there's no daylight at all. It's hard to keep track if this is night or day."

"How long has it been since we've slept?" Monica questioned, yawning from the feeling of exhaustion. "It seems like two days since we last got some rest."

"It's hard to believe, but it's only been fifteen or sixteen hours. All these new things that we're seeing and learning have made the time pass by very quickly." Summer stretched and then continued. "We'd better get some sleep after we eat. Maybe we can take a quick break and play some computer games."

"All right!" Jose smiled as they walked down the corridor to the "cafeteria". "That's what I like to hear. I'll bet that I beat all of you to the Jordanean Star System. If I trap the Glob first, then I win the game and save the Universe." Jose stood up as if he were ready to destroy the Glob itself, a computer animated monster that robs each planet of its life.

"No way," teased Steve. "First you have to learn the secret of a planet's life before you can even attack the Glob. You'll be destroyed without that knowledge."

"I already know the answer," Tykesha blurted out. All of her friends looked at her in disbelief as they sat down at the table. Tykesha looked at them in her moment of triumph. She smiled at each of them. They waited for her to tell them the answer but she remained silent.

Eclipse interrupted as he escorted the tray of strange dishes of food into the room. With the plates before them, the six youth began testing each strange-colored food. The youth stared in amazement as they saw the plate floating through the air beside him. They all wondered how he could have developed such power.

"This tastes like squash," Monica said as she eyed the pink-colored food with suspicion. She winced in disgust, causing her face to look grotesque. "I hate squash."

"Monica, you have to keep up your strength and obtain the vitamins, minerals and other nutrients that you need to stay healthy and strong."

Monica looked at Eclipse with disdain. "You sound just like my mom!"

"You must establish a balance of life, Monica, so that your physical body will protect you when you are in the environment of a new planet."

"This tastes like meat loaf!" Maria said excitedly as if she had not heard the conversation between Monica and Eclipse.

"Hmm..." Summer savored a bite of the "meat loaf", enjoying the taste of her favorite meat. "Eclipse, what do you mean to

50

establish a balance of life?" Summer took another bite of "meat loaf".

"All worlds with living things, like your planet and mine, are in balance. Your body and even the nerves of your body are in balance also. If you upset any part of that balance, either on your planet or in your body, problems begin to happen. Eventually, if the balance is sufficiently changed, a planet and a living thing are destroyed. The balance of my planet has almost been completely destroyed and my planet is dying as are my people beginning to die." Tears came into the soft eyes of their new-found friend.

"I'm sorry, Eclipse." Summer tried to comfort him, but without success.

There was silence during the entire meal, except for the automatic guidance system of the transporter as it occasionally gave an update of the distance from their destination in the same language that Eclipse had used to command the transporter. Just as they were ready to go, Eclipse floated in front of them and looked at each one seriously. "You must now go and get rest. We will be at our destination within two days."

"Two days!" cried Steve. "We calculated that it would take six months!"

Eclipse continued. "If distance and time didn't change we would have to travel for six months. But at the velocity we are going, space changes shape. It is almost like bending the branch of a tree into the shape of a "U". I just point the ship in the direction of the shortest distance across the "U" to get to our destination."

The teens looked at each other, momentarily disappointed at not being able to finish their computer game but excited about the prospect of arriving at a planet far away from their own. They returned to the main control room, entered their sleeping quarters, and within minutes were all sleeping soundly.

Eclipse entered the room to wake the youth up to complete their final training. The boys yawned and began to groan. "We just got to sleep, Eclipse. It's the middle of the night", Jose complained.

"You have been sleeping for ten earth hours, Jose, and we are getting very close to our destination."

The boys slowly got up and, after taking a quick bath, dressed themselves and went to eat their next meal. They were surprised to see the girls already eating. "Bananas!" Summer smiled as she pointed to a round, blue fruit. There was no further talk amongst the friends. They ate quickly and assembled by the computer in the main control room.

Eclipse entered the control room in time to see Summer and her friends finishing the study of the cycles that sustained life on a planet and the balance in every ecosystem. "I'm glad that you have finished. There isn't much time. We will slow down to the speed of light within two hours. After that time it will be only six earth hours until we are landing at the planet Magma."

This was the first time that he had mentioned the name of the planet where they were going. The six friends looked at the crystalline screen and saw the outline of a spiral galaxy whose form was rapidly enlarging. It was the first time after leaving the Milky Way galaxy that the surrounding space did not look like a typical dark night on earth.

Maria seemed bothered by what Eclipse had said. "Eclipse, why do you call the planet by the name of Magma? That means lava from a volcano."

Eclipse smiled, as he noted the knowledge that she had gained. "It is because there is still significant volcanic activity on all parts of the planet."

"Why do we need to know about the balance of life that exists in our own body?" Jose said, changing the subject.

Eclipse looked at all six teenagers. His face showed a great pain that they had never before seen, even when he thought of the sorrowful conditions on his own planet. "Jose, I see you have looked ahead at the last subject in your computer training. You must understand the balance that exists in your own body so that you may return to the transporter alive."

This announcement caused all conversation to stop. Horror and fear began to fill their hearts as they contemplated, for the first time, the possibility of not being able to return to their homes and families. Each was afraid to ask why. They knew that they would find out soon enough. Without further questioning, they returned to the computer and began their final study of the balance that exists in human bodies. They did not notice the tears in the eyes of Eclipse as he looked at each of them before leaving the main control room.

Steve looked up for a moment from the computer. He hadn't noticed that Eclipse had come back into the main control room where they were studying and had been carefully watching them as they learned about the balance of life in their bodies. He felt a little strange and he wondered why Eclipse was watching them.

Eclipse sensed his concern. "You are perhaps in the most important part of your study, Steve." The other teenagers looked up. Eclipse looked at each of his friends. "All of you will encounter many different kinds of plant and animal life in each of the biomes that you will enter. Some will look at you as their prey. There are many new kinds of bacteria and viruses on this planet. You must avoid touching anything that looks infected or sick. Your bodies have not developed a resistance to many of the things you will find there. The forces of these infections will overwhelm your own body defenses. You must not eat any plant, fruit or animal or drink any water on the planet either. I will provide each of you with a three-day supply of food and water. You must concentrate solely on obtaining the healthy plant and animal life that I tell you to get."

"Why can't we eat or drink anything on this planet?" Steve said, looking puzzled. His friends mirrored the same look.

"Most water is safe to drink. There are some water supplies that are contaminated with different kinds of viruses, bacteria and fungi. You won't have time to kill them by boiling any water. In fact, some of those organisms cannot be destroyed by boiling."

The youth finally understood what he was saying. Summer still looked puzzled. "I understand that, Eclipse, but why can't we eat the plants on that planet?"

"There is one final ecosystem that you must learn about. This is the ecosystem of your own central nervous system. You must learn how it operates normally. There are drugs in many plants on this planet as there are on your own planet. Many of the drugs cure diseases of all kinds. Many, however, upset the balance in the ecosystem of your central nervous system and will change the way you behave, think and feel. Some drugs will confuse your thinking so that you won't be able to find your way back to the transporter alive or respond quickly enough to the dangers around you."

Eclipse looked quietly into the eyes of each of the youth to make sure that his message was understood. The look of fear indicated that they had understood his warnings.

CHAPTER 5

Eclipse faced the control panel next to the computer where Summer and her friends had just completed their study of the balance that exists in the nervous system. He spoke commands to the computer and the transporter decreased to a velocity of ten thousand miles per minute. Eclipse spoke again and the picture of a sun appeared on the crystalline screen. The youth smiled. It seemed so much like the sun they were used to on earth. They could imagine its warmth and longed to be outside, feeling its rays bathe their skin.

"Look carefully at the left side of the screen," Eclipse said softly. "In a few seconds you will see our destination."

All eyes stared at the place Eclipse had indicated and waited. "There... there it is!" Summer said excitedly. She pointed to the exact spot on the screen. It was difficult to see. But the right half of the planet was illuminated and its left side was in darkness. The size of the globe increased rapidly and the interstellar transporter automatically began to decrease speed.

"It looks just like Earth," Summer said, her voice filled with memories of her family and planet.

"Eclipse, am I seeing things, or are there two moons revolving around that planet?" Monica looked carefully at two small satellites moving in the same direction that the planet Magma rotated.

"You are right, Monica. Each is about twice the size of your moon. They are four hundred and sixty thousand miles from the surface of the planet." By this time the planet and its satellites were in full view. The whiteness of the clouds and the deep blue color of its oceans caused tears to come into the eyes of each of the teens. In between the clouds was the distinct shape of continents. The absence of lights on the dark side of the planet suggested the lack of human presence. This realization filled them with the loneliness of shipwrecked sailors on a deserted island.

Eclipse continued speaking as they entered the atmosphere of Magma and silently passed through the clouds. "The atmosphere of Magma is identical to that of Earth and to my planet. It is the only planet of this solar system that has living things on it. The distance of Magma from its sun is perfect to support life."

The continents were now in full view and increasing in size. The interstellar transporter had slowed to a mere one hundred miles per hour. "Those continents look nothing like our continents on earth. Their shapes seem so funny."

Eclipse smiled at the comment made by Tykesha. "You should see the shape of the continents on my planet. It seems funny to you because you are so used to the way your continents look. But the cycles of life that operate on Earth, also operate here as well as on my planet."

"Where are we going to land?" Steve asked, looking at the crystalline screen.

"At the equator, there is a huge mountain, bigger than any on Earth. The mountain has the tropical rain forest biome. The mountain is so high that all biomes of your planet and mine are found on this one mountain." Eclipse floated closer to the screen and showed the youth the image of a large mountain that was growing larger by the minute. "There...to the right of this mountain is a ridge, almost identical to the ridge where I met you, except it is in a different biome. It is at the level of the taiga biome. All but one small section of the ridge is covered with huge pine trees. It is like a meadow. That will be a secure place from which you and your friends can go to each of the biomes and will give you the greatest safety."

Steve looked directly at Eclipse, wanting to ask him what he meant by the "greatest safety", but didn't have the courage to do so. He looked quickly away as Eclipse's soft glance pierced to the depths of his heart.

Somehow, Eclipse sensed his need. "We can stay for only three days on this planet. Remember, the defense factors of your body to the new bacteria, viruses and fungi have not been developed. If you touch any infectious agent, it will quickly spread from an infection to a disease. I have the means to combat any problem that you might have, if you return to the transporter within the three-day limit. If you delay longer than that, you will die before you get back to the transporter."

Fear continued to grow in the hearts of the youth. "Is there any other danger?" Maria asked.

"Yes, there is. Some of the animals are very large. There are carnivores, herbivores and omnivores. You should be aware by now that you could become prey of any carnivore on this mountain."

"How can we protect ourselves, and how can we get these animals back to the transporter without them eating us?" Steve looked concerned, as did the others, as he asked the question.

"I will provide you with a device that will...." Eclipse was interrupted by a warning signal from the control panel. "We are near landing. Be seated." Eclipse spoke more commands to the transporter's computer. The velocity decreased. The meadow could clearly be seen on the screen. Blue and purple-colored wild flowers were accented by the light-green color of the medium-sized thin blades of grass underneath them. As they neared the meadow floor, the thickness of the pine-trees surrounding the meadow gave the youth the feeling of a strong, dark-green wall which provided security from the dangers within the forest. The transporter came to rest and lights blinked on and off as Eclipse continued to speak commands to the computer. Just at that moment, they noticed a huge dark-colored bear entering the meadow. It stopped when it saw the transporter and quickly retreated to the edge of the meadow and watched the transporter suspiciously.

"That is a species similar to your grizzly bear- one of the most ferocious bears on this planet. That is one of the species that has disappeared from my planet."

"And just how are we supposed to get that bear to come in here?" Maria was beginning to feel doubtful about agreeing to help Eclipse.

"I will show you." Eclipse spoke a command and a small compartment opened silently. Inside was a small object that looked like a pen. The youths looked at each other questioningly as they saw this harmless-looking instrument. Eclipse concentrated on the pen and it began to lift into the air as if by some invisible force. He stared at the pen and it moved quickly toward him while the youth stared in disbelief. He then began to float toward the exit of the transporter and Summer and her friends followed behind. They walked through the metal door into the room where they had first entered the ship. They finally reached the door that led to the outside world. It opened automatically as they approached it. Stepping outside into the crisp, clean air, the youth looked behind them, expecting not to see the transporter. They gasped as the mammoth structure loomed at least a hundred and fifty yards into the air and well over three hundred yards from side to side and end to end. The sun reflected off of the metal-like outer covering of the transporter.

Jose wondered why it was so big. As the heat of the sun warmed their bodies, the six youth quickly forgot that they were on a new and dangerous planet. They began to run like wild animals having been recently released from captivity. The temperature was a warm seventy-five degrees. Thoughts of home and dreams of their mountain adventures with their families on Earth filled their souls with joy.

"Everyone return immediately!" Eclipse's voice was stern and had the impending feeling of disaster. The youth responded immediately and began to run toward the transporter. The grizzly bear had begun to advance on the group of frolicking teenagers. They had become the prey of a vicious predator that was fast approaching them.

"Stay where you are!" Eclipse warned. They froze in their tracks as they watched the bear running toward them. They realized that there was no way they could outrun the hungry animal. Eclipse quickly floated in between the youth and the bear. He caused his "pen" to point toward the bear and, as he spoke a command, a button on the pen was pushed. A beam of light shot from the tip of the "pen", hitting the bear in the head. It fell, stunned, then stood up slowly and raised itself on its hind legs, towering above them and roaring in anger. The bear suddenly disappeared.

Jose looked at Eclipse in bewilderment. "W...w...what happened? Where did the bear go?"

"Follow me and I will show you." He led the youth back into the transporter. The tree moved back and forth, greeting them as they entered the transporter. It looked three feet taller. As Eclipse passed the tree, he spoke to it with tenderness and its movements seemed to greet him in return with a human-like quality.

A different door than the one leading to the control room appeared. Eclipse walked through the metal door and the six youth followed. They entered an area of the ship that was gigantic. At the far end, they saw the grizzly bear resting peacefully on the metal floor. Surrounding the bear was a beam of light that served as walls to prevent the bear from escaping.

"Boy, what a stun gun. How did you do that?" Steve asked.

"This stun gun, as you call it, will transport anything into this large room and set up a living space for it to survive the journey to my planet. The computer determines the species of the plant, insect or animal and food is automatically prepared and sent through the ceiling into each room of light." The youth looked at Eclipse in disbelief. They were about to express their doubts when the ceiling opened up and a large piece of raw meat was lowered to the floor by a metallic hand. They watched the bear look around in bewilderment, slowly approach the meat and suspiciously sniff it. After a few seconds of looking at the meat, he eagerly began to tear it to pieces.

Eclipse continued his explanation: "All insects, birds, animals, trees and plants of any kind will be processed in a similar manner. This collection process will only work when the transporter is visible and within fifty kilometers of where you shoot the animal or plant."

"This is like a modern Noah's Ark," Summer interrupted.

Eclipse smiled and his eyes twinkled at her comment. He had studied the history of planet Earth. "That is right, Summer. And each of you will be the person who will seek out the living things."

"If we're going to be like Noah, then don't we need a member of the opposite sex for that bear?" Tykesha asked.

"Yes. You will need male and female of the species that are extinct on my planet. Vegetation can be obtained by getting the seeds or by shooting at the plant, itself."

"But what if that's a boy and the next grizzly bear we shoot is a boy, too?"

"The computer will automatically detect the sex of the animal, Tykesha. If it is the same sex, then the laser beam becomes a ray which causes the animal to freeze long enough to allow you to get away before it wakes up."

"That's cool, but are you sure it will work, Eclipse?" Jose looked at the small instrument with uncertainty.

"It worked that way on my planet and should work the same here." Eclipse seemed so sure that it momentarily quieted the fears of the youth. "It is time for you to start the sample collection. I will give you enough food and water to last three days. Remember, touch no animal or plant that looks like it may be infected. Don't get near any animal. If any gets near you, then use this instrument." He showed them the button that they needed to push to activate the laser beam. "I need specific plants, animals and insects from six of the eight biomes that are on this mountain. The only two biomes I need nothing from are the desert and ice cap biomes."

"How will we know what kinds of living things to get for you?" Steve asked.

Eclipse handed a green, crystalline rock and a "stun gun" to each person. "The crystal is a communicator which will allow you to talk to each other and to me. It also is a miniature computer that connects to the transporter's computer. You must get those items that are unique to each of the biomes. These are the living things that are disappearing from my planet." The youth put the communicator and "stun gun" into their pockets.

"Will you come with us, Eclipse?" Monica questioned.

"I must be here to decontaminate any infectious agent that comes with the material you send and to respond to any emergency that you may have. Since I need a sample of soil from each biome, I will have to be here to treat the soil in a special way in my laboratory so that the nitrogen-fixing bacteria can survive the journey. The nitrogen-fixing bacteria are disappearing from my planet and the nitrogen in my atmosphere is decreasing to levels that will threaten all life." Eclipse led them to another room where six backpacks loaded with provisions were stored. He began to assign each to a biome when the entire transporter began to rock gently back and forth. Each stood in silence, not knowing what was going on. The rocking increased. Suddenly, a strong jolt hit the ship, throwing the youth to the floor. Jose and Summer tried to get up, but the violent shaking of the transporter caused them to fall again. It felt like the transporter was disintegrating. In addition to the shaking ground, the loudest sound that the youth had ever heard came from deep within the surface of the planet. It was so loud that none of the youth heard Eclipse yell "Earthquake!" as he quickly left the room to save the transporter. He floated into the control room and spoke the commands that raised the ship above the ground. The shaking immediately stopped but the roar of the grinding earth underneath Magma continued. The six youth remained motionless on the floor. Fear gripped their hearts.

Little by little the sound decreased and finally disappeared. Eclipse set the ship back onto the meadow and quickly checked for damage to the transporter. Finding none, he returned to the room where he had left his friends. They still were laying on the floor when he entered the room. His look of concern troubled them as they slowly got to their feet.

"What was that?" Tykesha asked, still shaken from the experience.

"It was an earthquake," Eclipse explained. "You need to know one other thing. The mountain where you are going is an ancient volcano. I left sensing devices when I visited here last. During the last thirty earth days earthquake activity has increased tremendously. Magma from underneath the surface of the mountain was one thousand meters below the surface of the top of the mountain. After this earthquake it is now only two hundred and fifty meters from reaching the top. With the frequency and strength of the earthquakes, we may not have three days before this volcano explodes once again. The first explosion of this volcano was the most powerful one recorded on a planet in this sector of the universe."

"What will happen when it does blow its top?" Summer asked.

"When it explodes, fifty percent of the biomes on this mountain will disappear in seconds after the blast. The remainder will be destroyed within twenty-four hours from the lava that will come from the top of the mountain."

"Is there any other place in the universe where we can go to replace the missing species for your planet?"

"No, Summer. There is another planet in a galaxy near the Milky Way Galaxy that is about two hundred years from developing to the point of this planet. By that time, life on my planet will be gone." Eclipse looked saddened. He dared not ask the youth to embark on such a dangerous mission. He was about to tell them to return to the control room to go back to Earth, when Summer picked up a backpack, put it on her shoulders and walked toward the metal door.

"Wait a minute, girl!!" Tykesha ran to intercept Summer before she walked through the door. "Didn't you hear the man? We don't have three days. This mountain could be destroyed today with another earthquake like the one we just had." The transporter began to rock once again, as an after shock rippled through the ground, and then subsided. "There's another one Summer!! That probably changed the level of the magma again."

"We can do this! Eclipse's family and friends and whole planet are at stake." Summer set her jaw and continued to walk forward but Tykesha grabbed her and prevented her from moving.

"Summer, don't be stupid. We should never have let you go into the light in the first place. But this... this is pure suicide." Tykesha's eyes were filled with fear as she spoke. She looked at her friends to help her detain Summer, but they were frozen with indecision.

"Get out of my way, Tykesha! We've come too far not to try." Tykesha realized that it was impossible to change Summer's mind, so she let her go. Tykesha looked at Eclipse for support, but tears had filled his eyes as he realized just how good a friend that Summer really was.

"My instruments do indicate that there is at least a two day margin of safety, but beyond that, I can't guarantee anything."

"Eclipse, can we do it in two days?" Steve asked.

"It is possible, if you do not run into any difficulties. If you choose to go and an earthquake occurs, even if you have not completed gathering all the species I need, we must leave this planet immediately." Eclipse looked sternly, but compassionately at Summer. She nodded her head in agreement.

"The tundra biome will be closest to the top. I'm the fastest runner, so in case it blows, I might be the only one that can make it down in time... So we need to get...."

Eclipse interrupted Summer. "We won't have time to go to the chaparral biome. Steve and Jose, I want you two to go to the tropical rain forest biome together. That will be the most dangerous of them all in regards to the animals, plant life and parasites." Steve and Jose nodded their heads and began putting on their packs.

"Now wait a second," Maria interrupted, pointing to Tykesha and Monica. "Just because we're girls doesn't mean we can't handle danger."

Tykesha looked shocked at what her friend had just said. "Not so fast, girl. I have no intention of going to the tropical rain forest biome. Those bears don't look very friendly, either. I think I'll just stay here and help Eclipse."

Eclipse continued as if the girls had not said a word. "Tykesha, I would like you to stay here in the taiga biome." Tykesha was disappointed that she couldn't stay in the transporter but looked relieved that she wasn't going to travel too far from its safety. "Monica, you must go to the savanna biome and Maria, you will go to the temperate forest biome." The rest of the youth put the packs on their backs and left the transporter.

As they were walking toward the huge pine trees, the ground began to shake again. "We'll never make it out of here alive," Tykesha groaned. The others ignored her words, for the possibility of not returning to Earth and being killed on a planet so far away from home had already given them sufficient reason to worry. They entered the thick forest and followed the ridge until it met the mountain. The six youth separated after hugging each other and saying a silent prayer for their safety. Never before in their lives had they performed such an act to help another that would put their own lives in danger. As they walked on, a feeling of peace, courage and hope entered their hearts. It was a feeling unlike any other that they had ever known. Each silently contemplated the overwhelming odds against their success. As they continued walking, they thought of home and family, high school and friends, warm summer days and winter walks in the snow, the sound of birds in the spring time, flying kites, eating at fast food restaurants and going to many activities with their families.

CHAPTER 6

The ground shook again. Summer had lost track of the number of after shocks that had hit the mountain since she had begun collecting the samples that Eclipse had needed. Once again she looked toward the mountain. She was shocked as she saw the previously smooth incline of the mountain peak begin to form a bulge, as if a giant balloon was being blown up underneath the ground. The bulge appeared to be expanding rapidly. She blinked twice, looked away and then stared again to make sure that she wasn't imagining it. It was still growing! The bulge was on the right side of the peak of the mountain. After studying about the Mt. St. Helen's eruption, she knew that when it erupted that the force of the explosion would travel in the direction that the bulge was facing. She scanned the countryside in that direction and gasped. The interstellar transporter was less than three miles away, directly in the path of the impending eruption. She quickly took out the crystal communicator and began to speak quickly. "Eclipse, can you hear me?" No response. He's got to answer, she thought. "Eclipse, the volcano looks like it's close to eruption and you're right in the direction of the explosion!."

A moment of silence passed. Summer was just about to repeat the message when the voice of Eclipse sounded clearly. "Thank you Summer. You'd better get out of there immediately. My instruments indicate that if we have another strong earthquake that it will cause an eruption that will be one-hundred times more powerful than that which occurred at Mt. St. Helens. I will be taking off now and relocating to a ridge to the right of where you are located. There is a huge clearing that will serve as a good spot to for us to meet."

Summer looked to her right and strained her eyes. She didn't like what she saw. The huge clearing would add at least five miles for her return to the transporter. It also would require more walking for those who were at lower elevations. The transporter began to go into the air. "I see where you're going, Eclipse. Shall I contact the others?"

"No," Eclipse responded. "You do not have the capability of

simultaneously reaching all communicators. Your friends need to leave immediately and they need to hear that information now."

Summer put on her pack and began to run down the mountain. She heard Eclipse speaking in the communicator and describing where he was going, how to get there and warning her friends to leave immediately. Tykesha responded, followed by Maria and then Monica. There was no response from Steve and Jose. Eclipse called again to try to get them to respond. Moments of silence passed and nothing occurred. Summer watched as the transporter headed to the new landing site. Then, it deviated and headed toward the base of the mountain below her, where Steve and Jose had been working. She could no longer hear the voice of Eclipse. He was attempting to contact the communicators of Steve and Jose directly. Summer was breathing heavily as she continued her rapid descent but watched the transporter go slowly around the base of the mountain, disappear around the other face and reappear just under the growing bulge. She held her breath until the transporter cleared the path of the impending eruption. "Summer." She recognized the familiar voice of Eclipse in the communicator which she still held in her hand.

"I'm here, Eclipse. Did you locate Steve and Jose?" she asked, hoping that they had been found.

"I located Tykesha, Monica and Maria but found no signs of Steve and Jose." His voice seemed to be shaky and fearful.

"Would you have picked them up on your scanner if they were asleep or unconscious?" Summer held her breath for the reply.

"No, I would have seen them only if there was movement." The transporter was now continuing toward the new landing area. At that moment a large earthquake hit the area, causing Summer to fall and roll about twenty-five yards down the animal trail that she was following. Almost simultaneously, the bulge gave way and the force of fifty thousand atomic bombs was unleashed in an instant. Still on the ground, the edge of the shock wave passed her causing a momentary loss of her hearing. The force of air pushed her farther down the mountain. Had she been standing, the force of the wave would have carried her off of the mountain to certain destruction. She continued to roll down the side of the mountain and stopped only when her head struck a large granite boulder. Summer lay still, unconscious. She did not hear a second, unexpected explosion from the top of the mountain. This one occurred two minutes after the original blast and destroyed the other side of the mountaintop. Lava began to boil out of the caldera that had been opened by the blasts and to flow down all sides of the volcano. Ash was pouring heavenward, obscuring the early afternoon sun. Even though the sky was cloudless, bolts of lightning began to dart back and forth in the ash cloud and claps of thunder barked forth their announcement of the disaster.

Tykesha had to go down into a small valley as she walked quickly toward the new landing site. At the moment of the earthquake both she and Maria, who was about two thousand feet below her, were thrown to the ground. Maria was too low to see the results of the shock wave but she heard the deafening boom of the sudden and violent eruption of the volcano and also the second explosion. Unhurt, she stood and continued up the mountain. Tykesha, remaining on her stomach, looked up as she felt the rush of the wave go through the tops of the tallest trees of the valley floor. It was as if an airplane with a saw had rapidly gone through the tops of the trees and had cut them down with one blow. Hundreds of the heavy treetops and limbs began to fall to the ground. Before Tykesha could get up, a large treetop fell directly on her left leg. She cried in pain as it hit her. Stunned momentarily, she lay still as if the breath had been knocked out of her. The agony was almost unbearable. After a short time, she tried to turn over so she could move the tree off of her leg, but its weight was too much for her to move. She looked for the crystal communicator. It was on the ground beside her. Farther out, beyond her reach, was the stun gun that she had used to transport the animals, plants, soil samples and insects to the space ship. She grabbed the communicator and began to speak. "Eclipse, come in, I'm caught under a fallen tree. I need some help." Tykesha waited, but no reply came. She couldn't figure out what had happened. "Summer, come in, I need help. Are you there?" She waited a full two minutes, without a reply. She became nervous and began to feel thirsty from the pain in her leg. "Steve and Jose. Are you there?" No response. Eclipse had taught them that when she called the names of the people who had the communicators, a direct connection was made to that communicator but to none other. "Maria. Are you there?" She waited.

"I'm here, Tykesha. Is everything okay? That was some explosion. I guess the volcano has erupted."

Tykesha broke in. "I don't have time for talk. I'm hurt and need your help. No one else responds. Where are you?"

"I'm about four miles from entering the taiga biome and then I'm going to cut over through the valley that Eclipse described to us to get to the new landing site. Wait a minute Tykesha. Something is in the bushes behind me." Silence followed for what seemed to be forever. Finally, Maria's voice could be clearly heard, but it was obvious that she was panting.

"What's the matter, Maria?"

"It's okay. Monica just joined me and for a moment I thought she was a wild animal." Tykesha could hear a giggle in the background.

"It's not funny, Monica," Maria said, the communicator still on. "You scared me to death!"

"How could Monica catch up to you so fast?"

"She finished her specimen collection early and had started hiking back to the transporter. Where are you now, Tykesha."

"I'm in the valley . A large tree top is on my leg and I can't move."

"Hold on Tykesha. We should be there in about two hours or less."

"Two hours!" Tykesha murmured to herself. She wasn't sure if she would be able to withstand the pain much longer. The worst of thoughts began to cross her mind and she began to tremble with concern for the safety of her friends. What had happened to Summer, Eclipse, Steve and Jose? Were she, Monica and Maria the only ones left alive on this planet after the eruption? A sound interrupted her thoughts. She quickly turned her head to look behind her. A grizzly cub was walking down the trail and had spotted her. His curiosity had overcome his apprehension and he came right up to her and sniffed at her feet, then her hands and finally, her face. Tykesha froze in terror, not at the little cub but at the knowledge that she had gained that where a cub is, its mother was close by. She tried to grab for the stun gun. Her finger came to within a quarter of an inch. She tried again. A sharp pain in her leg caused her to cry out. The cub jumped back and ran away. Tykesha looked all around her to see if she could see the cub's mother. The sky above was growing prematurely dark. She could see the dark ash that she mistook for storm clouds. The thunder that she heard from the lightning above the top of the volcano made her shiver at the thought of being trapped in that position during a violent rainstorm.

Summer blinked open her eyes. She had only been unconscious for about thirty minutes, but she felt like it had been for days. She tried to get up but winced at the piercing headache that she had. She touched the area of her head that ached and discovered blood on her hands. Looking around in bewilderment, she searched for the transporter at the new landing site, but was now too low to see into the clearing. It seemed like it was night. Summer looked into the sky and blinked as light volcanic ash fell all over her. She looked up the mountain and was frightened by what she saw. A wall of slow-moving lava was flowing down on all sides of the mountain. Fresh lava continually splashed out of the caldera. Summer knew that if it had been a continual outpouring of lava that she probably would have been dead by now. She staggered to her feet and felt for her communicator and stun gun. She easily located the communicator, but the stun gun was missing. She looked all around the rock where she had been laying. There was nothing to be found. She had rolled down the mountain too far to make a search practical. It would take her over an hour to cover the area with no guarantees of finding the "weapon". I've got to keep going! she thought to herself. She saw her pack up the hill and walked slowly to get it. After putting the pack on, she continued down the mountain.

"Tykesha, come in, are you okay?" Summer held the communicator as she walked. The ash continually got into her hair and eyes and she finally had to stop and put a rag from her back pack over her nose and mouth to keep from inhaling the glass-like particles.

"No, I'm not okay." Tykesha said sarcastically. "I'm stuck

under a tree in the valley Eclipse told us to go through. And where were you a little while ago when I needed to hear your voice?"

"It's a long story. I'll tell you when I see you. I'm about forty-five minutes from you now."

"Hurry Summer, I can't reach the stun gun and there are grizzly bears in the area. Monica and Maria are together and won't be here for two hours."

"I'll get there first. There's probably some way I can get the tree off of your leg. I'm glad you still have your stun gun, Tykesha. I lost mine just a little while ago." A groan came from the communicator. Tykesha tried to make herself comfortable by piling up some pine needles as a pillow. She didn't notice the fungus growing on them as she laid her head on the pillow of pine needles. She had just begun to rest when the roar of a bear broke the stillness of the valley.

"Steve and Jose, are you okay?" There was no response. "Steve, please come in!" No sound came from the communicator. The rumbling of the bubbling lava seemed to increase dramatically. Summer turned to see what had caused the sudden change in sound. The golden-yellow lava liquid was now pouring steadily out of the top of the mountain. Steam came from the lava as it rolled faster down the slopes. Eclipse said that in twenty-four hours the mountain would be completely covered, she thought as she forced her legs to move faster. "Maria and Monica, where are you now?"

"About an hour from where Tykesha is, Summer. It's a hard climb, especially with all this black stuff falling from the sky. What is it?"

"Cover your mouths and noses. It's volcanic ash." Summer could hear Maria gasp for breath and Monica cough.

"Is there lava coming down the mountain?"

"Yes and very fast. So hurry or you won't make it. It's covering the entire mountain and destroying everything as it comes down."

Summer started running. She gritted her teeth as the pain in her head increased. She wanted to call Eclipse but was afraid that again she would get no reply. Finally, she had to try again! She called Eclipse, and then Steve and Jose, but no one answered her call. Hope slowly left her heart and she began to think that her decision to help Eclipse might result in their being stranded on this planet for the rest of their lives. She even doubted that Eclipse, Steve and Jose were still alive. Her mind raced uncontrollably with the fears that were now plaguing her. What if they caught one of the infections from the planet? It would only be a matter of a short time before each would suffer a painful death.

Her unconquerable will to succeed at all cost began to tell her that, no matter what, they would still be okay. Adrenaline began to stimulate her central nervous system and she ran with almost superhuman strength. Summer saw the valley ahead of her and she increased her speed. As she approached the bottom of the valley, she quickly stopped as if she had hit a brick wall. In front of her, a large grizzly bear was standing on its hind legs and growling in anger. Summer froze, afraid that it would see her and begin to chase her. Without her stun gun she would be no match for the animal. Then she saw Tykesha on the other side of the bear. She was close enough that Summer could see the fear in her eyes. Without thinking, she looked around, found a large rock and tossed it at the bear, hitting it in the head. The bear's growl became a roar of rage and it turned around to see who had attacked. Then Summer saw the baby cub and knew that she was in trouble. It was the mother bear. Spotting Summer, she got down on all fours and charged her. Summer sprinted back towards the volcano with the mother bear close behind. She could hear Tykesha yelling behind her to run faster. Somehow she had to lose the bear momentarily and return to obtain Tykesha's stun gun. That was their only hope. Summer almost tripped over two large treetops. The bear came closer. She turned quickly to the left and followed the width of the valley parallel to the volcano. The bear continued in pursuit. She jumped over a large treetop and turned left again. Somehow the bear had hesitated when she had gone over the fallen tree. This might just be the time I need, she thought. Summer looked to the left and in the distance could see the baby bear near Tykesha. Rapidly turning left again she increased her speed. Fifty yards.... forty..... thirty. Tykesha saw Summer running toward her and pointed where the stun gun was laying. Summer sprinted the last fifteen yards and grabbed the stun gun. She dropped to the ground and turned and pressed the button on the gun. The laser beam hit the mother bear in the head and she froze momentarily and then disappeared. Confused, she looked at Tykesha.

"That's the only thing I was unable to collect," Tykesha said, breathing heavily. They both looked at the baby bear who had seen its mother disappear. He began a tiny growl that sounded more like a cry.

"All right, little bear," Summer said as she pointed Tykesha's stun gun and activated the laser. The baby bear disappeared. "At least we know the transporter is visible and within fifty kilometers. I haven't been able to get in touch with Steve, Jose or Eclipse." Summer took the protective rag from her face and knelt down by Tykesha's feet to survey the situation. There was a large boulder near the tree top that covered Tykesha's leg, but it would not prevent the tree from being removed. There were other smaller, but very solid limbs that had broken off. Some were on top of the larger tree top. These limbs were heavy enough to cause Summer to groan as she removed them from the fallen tree top. Then she tried to lift the treetop from Tykesha's leg. "I can't move it!" she gasped in desperation. "We'll have to wait for Maria and Monica. Maybe the three of us together can lift this tree off your leg."

Summer took her communicator and called Maria and Monica to find their location. When she found that they were only fifteen minutes away, she was ecstatic. "My leg is getting numb" Tykesha complained. "I'm afraid that it's broken." Summer frowned and looked worried. The fifteen minutes seemed to take hours but at last Maria and Monica arrived. They hugged each other and then knelt down by Tykesha.

It was only then that Summer noticed the "pillow" that Tykesha was laying on. "Tykesha, those pine needles look infected."

The sparkle in Tykesha's eyes left. "Does that mean that I'm going to die?"

"Of course not," Monica comforted her as she removed the rag from her own face. "Remember that Eclipse said he had everything in the transporter to treat any diseases we get. They both turned to the job at hand. The three girls grabbed the treetop and lifted with all of their strength. It still did not move.

Suddenly animals of all kinds came running down the trail from the direction of the volcano. Rabbits, deer, and many smaller animals rushed past them as if they were oblivious of their presence. "They must be trying to escape from the lava coming down the mountain." Summer pointed to the red glow of the lava in the distance. She felt a wave of sadness come over her as she realized that it was now too late to go and find Steve and Jose without losing her own life. Her thoughts suddenly were interrupted as she saw four or five mountain lions running towards them from the volcano. She thought nothing of this until the mountain lions stopped as they got closer to the four girls. Now that they were closer they could see that there were six mountain lions in all. They began circling them and growling and slowly approaching them.

"Do you get the feeling that we're the prey here?" Tykesha said, her voice shaking.

"Monica and Maria, do you have your stun guns?" Summer asked. Monica shook her head, indicating that it had fallen and disappeared into a rapid stream of water as she was crossing it. Maria slowly removed hers from her pack and Summer carefully picked up Tykesha's. They aimed them at the two closest mountain lions and pressed the buttons. The mountain lions froze and then fell to the ground. They aimed at the next two and the laser beams shot out. The final two had seen the others freeze like statues and fall to the ground. They had already started charging the girls. They were only three feet from them and had leaped into the air when the laser beams hit their heads, producing the same result as with the other mountain lions, except that these two hit the three girls, knocking them on top of Tykesha. The force of the collision knocked the stun guns from the hands of the girls and, as they fell, the guns forcefully hit the soft earth and disappeared under the topsoil.

"Get off of me!" Tykesha complained to her friends. Tykesha, still on her stomach, was now covered by her three friends, who were in turn covered by two large mountain lions. Although they were large animals, the three girls used their hands and feet to push the mountain lions off. Tykesha sighed in relief and winced in pain at the same time as her three friends got up. Together, they dragged the two mountain lions farther away from her.

"Maybe we can pull the tree top off of your leg in the same way." Tykesha's three friends went to the end of the tree and started pulling with all their strength. The tree started moving. Tykesha screamed in pain as the tree rubbed over her already sensitive, but numb leg. "It won't work. We've got to lift it up and drag you out from under it before these lions wake up. Where did I put Tykesha's stun gun?" Summer frantically looked all around.

"Mine is gone too." Maria began to sob.

"You must have dropped them when the lions hit you. Maybe you dragged the lions on top of the stun guns." Tykesha pointed to where the mountain lions lay, motionless. The girls went over to one of the animals and began to drag it farther away. As they did, it began to stir and growl. They quickly dropped its legs and ran back.

"We have to figure out a way to get you out of here quickly, or we're all animal meat," Summer frowned as she spoke.

Summer looked around where Tykesha laid. She studied the large boulder near Tykesha's feet. Then she looked at the long, thick limbs that she had moved off of the treetop that had their friend trapped. She began to smile and then said, "Monica and Maria, do you remember Mr. Willow talking about levers in our science class in eighth grade?"

Monica quickly looked at the boulder. At the same time, Maria jumped up and ran toward the thick limb by Tykesha's leg. "The boulder can be the fulcrum!" Maria exclaimed with renewed hope.

Summer and Maria placed one of the large limbs on top of the boulder near Tykesha's leg while Monica guided the end of the limb under the tree top. The two girls began pushing down with all of their force. Monica readied herself, to pull Tykesha from under the weight of the tree. At first the tree did not budge. Summer and Maria selected a longer limb so that the fulcrum point could be changed, giving the girls greater lifting force. One of the mountain lions began to move and growl as if it were waking up. They began to push down again. This time, the heavy treetop began to move. "It's starting to lift off my leg!" Tykesha cried in pain. The lifting continued.

"Now, Monica!" Summer yelled as she and Maria gave a final, mighty push on the lever, allowing their full weight to rest on the end that they held. Monica pulled Tykesha's hands and slowly dragged her leg from under the tree. Suddenly, Summer's hands slipped and the tree crashed to the ground, pushing Maria back away from the lever. The tree barely missed Tykesha's foot. Summer almost collapsed, thinking that she had hurt her friends, but relaxed as she saw that Tykesha's leg was free and Maria was picking herself up off of the ground.

"Quick, let's get out of here!" Summer said tensely as she made a last attempt to find the stun guns. They still could not be found. Now, one of the mountain lions was attempting to get up so she stopped looking. She quickly ran to help Maria lift Tykesha off of the ground. They got on either side of her and began carrying her toward the clearing, still some two miles distant. Monica picked up her and Tykesha's backpacks and followed closely, walking as fast as she could. They could see the red glow of the lava and burning forest behind them and continually moving closer. The lava had set fire to the trees and the taiga biome was quickly being consumed. As Summer glanced back she saw that the fire had begun to enter the place where Tykesha had been trapped. The mountain lions were covered by the thick smoke that preceded the advancing flames.

An hour and a half had passed. Summer and Maria, who had continued carrying Tykesha without a break, were pushed forward by the advancing flames and lava behind them. Monica was becoming fatigued by the weight of the two backpacks. "We should be near the clearing, shouldn't we?" Tykesha said, her face filled with pain. She looked at her friends, hoping that she could find somewhere to lay down and rest.

"I hope so," Monica said breathlessly. "We all need a rest." The forest was thick around them, but they still could navigate by checking the position of the sun that was now near the horizon and occasionally shined through the spaces in between the trees as they continued to walk. The forest around them was now filled with large amounts of smoke. The girls began to choke and cough. They stopped momentarily and each took a drink of the water that Eclipse had provided for them. Summer, Maria and Monica soaked four rags with some of the water and placed three of them around their own faces. They tied the last one securely around the face of

Tykesha. Picking up their backpacks and Tykesha, they continued in the direction of the clearing. After an additional thirty minutes of walking, the trees began to decrease in density. They finally emerged into a clearing about a mile from side to side. As they left the wall of trees, all four began to look for the interstellar transporter. A beautiful meadow stood before them. The shadows of the large pine trees on one side of the meadow covered at least three quarters of the meadow itself as a result of the low angle of the hazy afternoon sun. They looked in every direction.

"I wonder why this meadow is right here?" Monica mused.

"Succession!" Summer smiled at her friends as she demonstrated the knowledge that she had gained during the journey to Magma. No one was impressed.

After a short time, the girls became serious and silent. They realized that the transporter was nowhere to be seen. "Maybe its invisible," Tykesha said hopefully.

Hearing the crackling of the burning forest behind her, Summer walked over to Tykesha and, without responding to her friend's comment, indicated to Maria and Monica that they needed to carry Tykesha farther into the large meadow. "Whether it's invisible or not," Summer finally said as they started walking, "we have to get to the middle of this meadow to protect ourselves from the fire." She looked back and saw that the lava was relentlessly continuing down the slope toward them.

As they traveled they came to numerous deposits of water, almost like the bogs that they had studied about on the transporter. In fact, except for the forest edge, the entire meadow was dotted with the water that had difficulty seeping into the ground. Finally they arrived at the center of the meadow and, finding a relatively dry spot, sat down and took some food out of their backpacks. Summer and Maria looked at Tykesha's face. They noticed that the whole side of her face that had touched the infected pine needles was inflamed and covered with the growing mycelia of a fungus. They motioned to Monica who audibly gasped as she saw the infection covering Tykesha's face. They dared not tell Tykesha. Without the transporter and Eclipse, they knew that the fungus would soon kill their friend.

"Do you think that animals will come here for protection from the fire?" Tykesha looked worried as she asked the question.

"We'll cross that problem when we come to it. There's no need to worry about something that hasn't happened yet." After speaking, Summer took out her communicator. "Eclipse, can you hear me? Monica, Maria, Tykesha and I are in the middle of the clearing where you told us to go. Where are you?"

The four girls waited for a reply but none came. Summer put the communicator near her mouth once again. "Jose, do you hear me?" No response. "Steve, are you okay? Please answer! Someone please answer!" No answer came.

Summer tried to hold back the sobs of despair that were swelling within her, but was unable to do so. Monica and Maria came over to Summer and tried to comfort her. Tears began to fill their eyes, too. Tykesha was tormented by the pain in her leg and now could feel the strange new burning sensation on the side of her face. She assumed that it was related to her severe leg pain.

"Summer, are you there?" The voice of Eclipse sounded loudly in her communicator.

So relieved from hearing the sound of Eclipse's voice, the four girls broke into cries of joy and continued sobbing uncontrollably. Summer put the crystal close to her mouth. "Y..y...yes we're here. Where have you been, Eclipse? I'm afraid Steve and Jose are both dead. Tykesha is hurting badly and we are waiting in the middle of the clearing." Her words were all mixed up and the flood of tears continued.

"Just calm down, Summer." It was Steve's voice. The tears came more freely than ever before. They could not say anything more because of the joy they felt hearing Steve's voice. "Thanks to Eclipse, Jose and I are okay."

The reassuring voice of Eclipse was then heard. "We are back on the transporter and will be there in less than ten minutes, Summer." Eclipse paused and waited for a break in the tears. When one came, he continued. "Summer, I'll never forget what you and your friends have done for me and my people. You are true friends." The girls managed to smile through their tears of joy.

Eclipse spoke again, but this time with nervousness in his voice.

"I'm detecting five or six areas of motion from the edge of the clearing heading your way. You had better get your lasers out, just in case they are predators."

Monica and Summer stood up and looked all around them. They could see the faint outline of mountain lions rushing toward them. "Bad news Eclipse," Summer quickly reported. "We've lost our stun guns and those are hungry mountain lions that are charging us. Can you hurry?"

"We'll be over you in two minutes."

"They'll be here in less time than that!" screamed Monica into Summer's communicator. Tykesha looked into the darkening sky for signs of the transporter but none appeared. The mountain lions were only one hundred yards from them and closing rapidly. Summer quickly looked into her pack and found a small knife, grabbed it and stood motionless. Maria and Monica found their knives and stood close to Summer. The animals covered the entire distance in less than thirty seconds. They did not stop as they had done before. They had been angered by the effect of the stun guns. Summer met the first mountain lion, nearly five times her weight. She lunged at the cat and stabbed the animal in the chest. The blade was not long enough to do anything but enrage the animal even more. It lashed out with its claws and caught Summer across her legs, tearing her jeans to pieces. She fell to the ground in excruciating pain, blood covering her shredded jeans. A second animal had lunged at Monica and had grabbed her left hand in his teeth as she gashed its face with her knife. He roared in pain and let go of her hand. The hand was pierced with teeth marks and bloody. The lion jumped up on her and pushed her down to the ground. The mountain lion that was closest to Maria sprang into the air and pushed her onto her back. As he raised his paw, Maria readied her knife. The paw fell like lightning and Maria's knife cut a big gash in the side of his leg. It was not enough to deter the lion, as he gashed her chest and stomach deeply with his claws. Tykesha was unable to grab her knife and knew that in her weakened condition would be no match for the animals. But she found several stones near where she lay and began throwing them as hard as she could at the mountain lions who were attacking her friends. She squarely hit them as well as two others as they attempted to come near. They backed off momentarily, but with renewed fury approached the girls once more. Summer, Maria and Monica realized that they did not have the strength to prevent another attack.

Laser beams began coming from the sky, hitting four of the closest animals and causing them to drop to the ground. The girls could see that they were momentarily stunned. But now, as they watched the transporter come closer, they realized that they had been sufficiently injured to the point of not being able to get up and walk into the transporter itself.

"Eclipse, thank you." the gratefulness in her voice was reward enough for Eclipse. "I don't think any of us are capable of standing up." From her peripheral vision, Summer caught additional motion near them and painfully turned her head only to see two other mountain lions approaching them. "More lions are coming for us!" Summer screamed.

The girls suddenly felt light and their bodies were being raised from the ground by an invisible force that came from the interstellar transporter. The two mountain lions lunged into the air, barely missing them. The girls continued to rise, and as they reached the transporter, they passed through the metallic outer shell of the ship.

The next thing that the girls remembered was Steve, Jose and Eclipse looking down at them. They blinked their eyes and looked around. Again they were in another area of the transporter that they had never seen. It looked somewhat like a hospital room. Summer looked at Steve. "What happened to you and Jose?"

"If it wasn't for Eclipse, we would have been dead. Once we finished our sample collections we started hiking up the mountain. As we walked under this canopy of trees a huge snake dropped on us and started to try to break our bones. We barely had enough time to get our stun guns out. We zapped the snake and it was out like a light. As we got up from under the weight of the snake we noticed that its entire outer scale was covered with pus. The pus was all over our arms and necks. We didn't think much about it and continued up the mountain. It wasn't three hours later that we knew that we were in trouble. We had really high fevers and were beginning to get dizzy. Then we just passed out and don't remember a thing until we woke up on the transporter."

All three girls looked curiously at Eclipse. He sensed their question. "After the mountain exploded, I managed to keep the transporter from being destroyed. I watched as almost the entire ice cap on the top of the mountain melted and flooded a valley on the opposite side from where you were working. The blast itself had leveled all of the forest in the area where we first landed. I continued to look for Steve and Jose. I made one more circle around the volcano and after detecting no movement, I decided to send a reflecting signal to their communicators to try and locate them in case they were unconscious. That is how I found them."

"But what about the diseases you had. You look perfectly normal now?" Summer still felt disoriented from her ordeal with the mountain lions. Steve and Jose looked at Eclipse to fill in this part of the story.

"The terrain was too rough for me to land the transporter so I caused it to automatically hover while I used the beams to allow me to go to the ground. I found them both unconscious with high fevers and with a virulent bacteria eating away their flesh. About fifty percent of their faces and necks had begun to deteriorate."

The girls recoiled at the gory picture that was painted for them. After the initial shock, they looked again at the boys. "But they're perfectly normal now. Just look at...."

Eclipse interrupted Summer. "The vaccines that I brought with me to the surface of the planet were designed to heal that as well as the fungal infection that Tykesha had." Summer, Maria and Monica quickly looked at Tykesha. Her face also was disease-free. They then stared down at their own bodies, knowing the severity of the wounds that they had received. Their skin was completely healed. Even Summer's jeans did not have a rip in them. Tykesha could move her leg without pain. "You girls looked as bad as did these boys when I first saw them. It took several hours to decontaminate them and to return them to their normal state. Then we came aboard the transporter. That is when I called you."

"But why couldn't we communicate with you when you were helping the boys?" Tykesha looked carefully at Eclipse as she asked him the question.

80

"I had left my communicator on the transporter. Whenever I use reflecting beams to locate someone, it always inactivates the communicator so I could not hear any of your calls or use theirs to call you."

"How long have we been here in this room? Are we still on Magma?"

"Only six hours," blurted Jose. "We're heading toward Earth! Our mission was successful! Eclipse has gained enough samples to repopulate his planet so it won't die!"

Hope re-entered the heart of Summer and her friends. They excitedly began talking about the prospects of seeing their families once again and to start high school when they returned. They didn't see Eclipse grow uneasy. Finally Eclipse interrupted the happy group of teenagers.

"There is only one small problem about your return to Earth," Eclipse said, almost apologetically. The group of youth visibly became tense, waiting for what he had to tell them but not wanting to hear.

"With space travel just beyond the speed of light, it is fairly easy to calculate how to go back in time so that you can return to your planet at the same time that you left it. I was first to develop the transporter concept. This transporter travels many hundreds of thousands of times the speed of light. It is more difficult to pinpoint precisely at what time period of Earth's history we will arrive at, especially after traveling that fast. The computer can only make a rough estimation and its program did not include a correction factor for the additional weight of the samples you collected."

The silence that came over the teenagers was so intense that it could be felt, like a cool mist of fog. They looked at Eclipse in disbelief. Jose was the first to speak. "Let me see if I understand what you're telling us. While we're traveling at or beyond the speed of light, we actually age differently than do those on our planets?" Eclipse nodded and Jose continued. "Then we get older than they do or do they get older than we?"

"At the speed of light, those on our planets get older. Well beyond the speed of light like we are traveling, ...well, we are the first to do it."

CHAPTER 7

The youth could not believe that they might live the rest of their existence in some remote prehistoric era or some futuristic society. In either situation, they would be without their families. "This would only be temporarily," Eclipse explained, sensing their concerns. "I need to get back to my planet as soon as possible. I will leave each of you with a communicator. Steve and Jose, I have repaired yours. Never go anywhere on your planet without it. If you are not in the appropriate year of Earth's history, contact me directly. The communicator will reach all areas of the universe. When I have completed my mission, I will enter the appropriate settings in the transporter's computer and return you precisely to the time when I first took you with me."

"But how long will we have to wait if we aren't in the correct time?" Tykesha asked, frowning.

"Once I have completed my mission, I can create the computer program that will allow me to return at precisely the same time of my leaving you on the ridge. That is, of course, if I do not have to travel too far beyond the speed of light. If that were the case, then it might be between two to four months after leaving you on the ridge." Tykesha groaned and the others silently felt distressed inside. The possibility that they might have to live in a strange time period even for more than a week or two seemed almost unbearable to them.

The six youth looked at each other and shrugged their shoulders. "Why can't we go with you?" Summer asked. "It seems that we would be safer than in a society that might treat us as aliens ourselves. If we arrived when we were in elementary or junior high school, we still couldn't return home. It would be too much of a shock for our parents to see us as teenagers with a younger version of us sitting by them."

"I am ninety percent sure that I will get you back to within ten years after the time you actually left. The chance that you could be living in a futuristic world is remote. It is a very small chance that we will arrive anywhere prior to the time that you left with me."

Eclipse seemed very confident about what he said. The youth decided not to challenge his statement. They just hoped that their return would not be disastrous and that they would see their families once again.

The alarm on the control panel sounded. Eclipse took one look and spoke a command which put their own solar system on the crystalline screen. The transporter was automatically slowing for its approach to planet Earth and the size of the earth was rapidly growing. As Summer and her friends saw the familiar view of their home planet, their worry increased. It almost seemed like an alien planet to them, now. They felt somewhat like orphans in a cold, immense universe.

"Look, lights on the dark side of the planet!" Steve cried with renewed hope in his voice. "At least we're not in a prehistoric time period." As they passed silently through the clouds that covered the western half of the North American continent, they saw the familiar outline of the United States. The transporter slowed even further. Steve continued speaking. "Are we invisible, Eclipse?"

"Yes we are, Steve." He did not respond further, but continued speaking commands to the computerized control center. The seven watched as the familiar sight of Mt. Walamalee came into view. The ridge became larger and larger until the transporter came gently to rest on the surface of the ridge. After checking his scanning equipment, Eclipse continued. "It looks like we are definitely here at some time after we had left on our journey."

"How can you tell, Eclipse?" Maria asked. She walked closer to the crystalline screen.

"There is still a group of tents that were placed by the group that sent the probe into the transporter. It looks abandoned. There are no life forms near us at all." Eclipse looked at his six friends. "I will miss you and never forget you. If you need me, I will come back. You had better get ready to leave the transporter. I will deactivate the invisibility device in the next five minutes."

The six youth hesitated. They did not want to move quickly, for as they looked at Eclipse, they saw tears of sincere gratitude in his eyes. Summer approached him and stood on a chair and gave him a kiss on the cheek. Then, one by one, each came and hugged him.

84

They smiled and returned to their quarters to obtain the items that they had brought with them. Then they returned to the control room. "Take this pack of food in case you cannot get back to your homes. There is enough concentrated food that will last the six of you at least one month, if necessary."

Steve accepted the pack, put it on his back and they walked through the door to the room that they first entered as they came through the red-blue light. The tree was much taller now and it still waved back and forth.

Overcome with curiosity, Monica asked, "Is that really a tree or is it an intelligent life form from another planet?"

Eclipse smiled. "This came from Magma. I got it the first time that I was there and identified Magma as the place where I should obtain the material to save my planet. It is the only species of tree that responds to a high degree when other living things are present. I had brought it with me to keep me company on my journey."

As the youth neared the door of the transporter, it automatically opened. Instead of the foreboding of Magma, the familiar sight of home greeted them. They stepped off the transporter, turned one more time and waved good-bye to Eclipse. As they walked toward the trail that led to the meadow where they had camped, they glanced back often. They saw the transporter disappear. They neither heard nor saw the transporter from that point on.

Summer reached for her communicator and spoke. "Eclipse, good-bye dear friend."

"Thank you. You are courageous and faithful friends." Eclipse's voice was loud and clear. They all felt safer once they knew that the communicators still worked.

The familiar trail led down the mountain. As it disappeared into the pine trees, they noticed the tent city that had been created by the military personnel. As they came closer they sensed something different. In the late morning sunlight, it was clear that these tents had been there a long time. A few had collapsed and the tent material itself seemed terribly worn.

"I wonder what happened here?" Summer commented.

"They probably used old tents. You know the military. Always trying to recycle their used material." Even with Steve's comment, the youth felt uneasy at the aged appearance of the camp. They continued speedily down the trail and within forty-five minutes emerged into the beautiful meadow that was near the campsite that they had left only a short time previously. They walked through the camp area and then continued down the road which led to the mouth of Lambs Canyon.

"Did you notice something different back there at the camp?" Tykesha asked.

"The grass seemed a little tall." Jose said indifferently. "I didn't notice anything else."

Tykesha pressed her point. "I mean about the campsites themselves. Especially the fire pits." Everyone looked at Tykesha strangely. No one had noticed any difference. Tykesha felt embarrassed at having made the comment and felt like she was a little paranoid noticing that the fire pits appeared not to have been used for years.

They continued walking silently down the road. They came to a huge tree that had fallen and blocked the road so no traffic could pass. They didn't think anything about it until they passed another tree that had similarly blocked the road. This time they stopped and looked at the base of the fallen tree.

"It doesn't look like it's been cut. In fact, the charred part on the bottom makes it appear like this one may have fallen when it was struck by lightning." Maria seemed puzzled.

Steve examined the next tree farther down the road. "This looks the same. That series of thunderstorms must've really been damaging to the forest."

The six walked on for over four hours. The paved part of the road had many potholes in it. "I don't remember all of these holes being here," Summer remarked. The others hadn't remembered them either. Because it had been so well traveled, they had repaired any holes in the road that had occurred from the freezing and thawing cycles of the previous winter. "It's almost like we've arrived here after one really rough winter and the road crews haven't yet come to repair the road."

"If that's the case, Summer, then where's the snow. If you remember, there was none on the ridge, or on the top of Mt.

Walamalee." Maria's comment caused an increased apprehension within each of her friends. Although it was familiar-looking, it just didn't feel the same.

"Shouldn't we be near the interstate by now?" Monica questioned.

"I think so, Monica. It should be about a mile after that turn down there or my name isn't Steve. There should be some cabins up there also." The little group walked on, but at a slower rate. "I wonder what time of year and what time of day it is? It must be at least sixty-five degrees out now. That could put us in the fall of the year. Based on the angle of the sun, I would say that it's about three-thirty or four o'clock in the aftern...."

"Steve, your analyzing things too much," Summer interrupted. "Let's wait until we get back to our homes and then we can ask all those questions and, hopefully, get a few answers. Besides, I feel weird enough already."

They rounded the bend and came to a group of cabins. As they neared the dirt roads which led to the cabins they noticed that the windows of the cabins had been broken and many were boarded up. Graffiti covered the boards on the lower windows. Their mouths dropped open. Broken bottles of beer, old tires, empty cartridges of guns, and piles of garbage dotted the lots of each cabin. Each of the youth tried to ignore the obvious feeling of impending fate that was quickly overpowering them. Slowly, they turned and continued walking toward the interstate, not knowing what they would find.

Within twenty minutes they could see the mouth of the canyon in the distance. They started walking faster, avoiding the increasing numbers of pot holes in the road.

"Do you hear what I hear?" Jose asked. They all stopped and listened carefully.

"I don't hear a sound," Tykesha said after a moment. "The mountains are supposed to be quiet."

"Not at the interstate, Tykesha." Then it dawned on everyone that there was absolutely no sound of roaring engines from trucks or cars whizzing by the mouth of the canyon.

They started running. Finally the mouth of Lambs Canyon was in full view. A large, barbed wire fence covered the entire entrance

87

to the canyon. There wasn't even a gate in the fence itself. However, there was a large sign facing the interstate. They were unable to see what it said.

What surprised the youth most was the large quantity of traffic that was traveling on the interstate. The only thing that was missing was the sound of the engines of the cars. They glided along effortlessly and silently. Only the whining sound of the tires moving along the road could be heard. The eyes of the youth widened even farther. On the opposite side of the interstate were large apartment complexes in an area that had previously been filled only with forest. These complexes filled the mountains as far as the eye could see, from east to west.

"I think we're somewhere in the future," Maria said, looking visibly upset. She started to cry.

"It might not be very far in the future." Jose tried to comfort Maria. "I remember my eighth grade teacher talking about a population explosion that was expected during the Winter Olympics that were to be held in the Salt Lake area in the year, two thousand two."

"None of us are going to find the answers to our questions until we get on the other side of that fence!" Summer's voice seemed determined. She began to walk closer to the fence to see if there was a way to get over without cutting themselves on the barbed wire on top. The others followed her, looking up and down the fence line to try to find a way to get out.

"There's a small opening between the fence and the rock at the right over there," Monica said, pointing to the area. "We'll have to cross the stream to get there though."

They looked at every other area of the fence. The small opening was the only way to get out, but it was so tiny that they weren't sure that they could make it. After crossing the stream, they approached the small opening. Their fears were confirmed when they saw that only a small animal could make it through. Steve looked at the fence as it ended into the side of a large, steep hill. "I'll bet that if we climb this hill, we can slide down on the other side and get out of here."

They looked at each other for a moment and nodded agreement.

The slope where they now stood was too steep to climb, so they retreated back up the canyon until they found an area that was better suited for climbing. It wasn't long before they had arrived at the top. When they came to the edge where the large hill steeply dipped down to the interstate, Jose smiled and said, "This is going to be just like it was when we were kids and slid down that steep water slide in Provo." The others smiled, sat down and pushed themselves down the side to the bottom. They made it in record time, unawares that they had broken a laser beam and video security system at the top of the hill. A silent alarm sounded in a military outpost less than three miles up the interstate toward the east.

Once at the bottom, the youth quickly walked to the sign on the fence. The sun had gone behind the western mountains, but the words on the sign were still clearly legible. "WARNING: NO TRESPASSING- By order of the United States Government." Then in much smaller print at the bottom it read, "This is a restricted area. Any unauthorized entry will result in arrest and prosecution."

After reading the contents of the sign, Summer spoke softly, "Do you suppose it was closed because we disappeared into the light?" They turned around and faced the busy interstate. "I bet we could get at least one person living in all of those apartments over there to make a telephone call or two for us." Summer walked closer to the interstate to attempt to cross, but the steady stream of traffic and the wideness of the interstate made it too difficult.

"Let's just walk toward the city. It's about twenty miles and maybe someone might pick us up," Steve said as he began walking west along the side of the interstate freeway. The others followed him.

They hadn't walked more than two hundred yards when they heard the sound of sirens coming from behind them. Stopping to see what was the matter, they looked and saw two military trucks led by three Highway Patrol cars. Intrigued by the unusual nature of this sight, the six youth watched. Cars on both sides of the freeway were pulling over to the side and stopping. Some narrowly missed hitting the watching youth. Darkness was beginning to increase in the sky.

The caravan came nearer, and to the surprise of the little group of youth, the five vehicles crossed over the center of the freeway and headed directly towards them. They all looked behind them to see who they were chasing but couldn't see anything suspicious. The five vehicles silently surrounded the six youth. Soldiers jumped out of the trucks and pointed their rifles at them. Astonished, they found themselves unable to move. The three police officers came through the wall of soldiers and carefully approached the nervous teenagers. Their eyes were wide with surprise and their emotions were mixed with disbelief and fear.

"What were you kids doing on that hill back there?" one of the police officers called out gruffly.

It finally dawned on the youth that they were the "fugitives". They realized that they must have tripped off some invisible security system. Steve tried to give them a reply. "Well, sir, you see, we couldn't get out of the canyon over the fence, so we decided to climb that big hill and slide down to the freeway.

"That's impossible," one of the soldiers holding a gun yelled. He had Sergeants stripes on the side of his uniform. "There's no way you could have come from the other side. That whole area has been sealed for years. Just how did you get there?"

Summer suddenly became bold. "We came from the ridge just below Mt. Walamalee. And just why are you pointing those guns at us?"

An additional army vehicle drove up. It too, made no noise except for the crackling of the tires over the rocks on the side of the road. A man who wore the uniform of an army officer got out and went to the soldier who had yelled at Steve. His words to the soldier and the soldier's reply were muffled but every once in a while a word could be clearly heard. "Sergeant Fargo...video.......top of hill.......truth......six....." At the end of the conversation, the Sergeant commanded the others to be dismissed. All the soldiers were soon in the backs of the trucks. The three Highway Patrolmen went to work to clear the congestion of traffic that had occurred. The officer and the Sergeant came close to the group of teenagers. They stared at each one, then pulled out a photograph and looked at it. Their eyes grew as large as saucers. "Well, I'll be..." said the officer. He did not identify himself to the youth. "Tell me again how you got here?"

Summer explained what she had just said before he had driven up.

"Then how did you get to the ridge without being detected?" he asked. "We have the same kind of security system that you went through all around that entire area. All incoming roads from other canyons have been sealed." He stopped and looked at Summer. "And what is your name, young lady."

"Sir, I'd be glad to give you my name if I knew yours and why your men treated us so rudely."

"I'm sorry. My name is Colonel Groundwater. I'm in charge of a special investigative mission of six teenagers who disappeared over twenty years ago on the ridge you came from today. Once the six youth disappeared and efforts to find them failed, the entire area was sealed. The special video and laser security was placed all around after a lot of vandalism occurred to ensure that no one would disturb the area. I recently took command of this project last month."

"What year is it, Colonel Groundwater?" Steve asked politely.

Once again, the Colonel took out the photograph and looked at it again. Then he looked at Steve. He shook his head slowly. "It's almost two thousand sixteen. In another year, the entire area was to be reopened to the public if no progress had been made in locating the youth. Could you possibly be the missing teenagers?"

"Colonel Groundwater, my name is Summer Solstice. We are your missing teenagers." Summer put her hand out to shake his hand. His arm was so weak, he hardly had the strength to take Summer's hand.

The Colonel stood, motionless. He didn't speak for a long time as he went first to Summer, then to Steve, then to Jose, to Tykesha, then Maria and finally Monica. He looked at each face individually, then again at the photograph in his hand. It was then that he finally spoke, "I don't understand it. You haven't aged a bit in the last twenty years. How can it be?"

Jose interrupted. "Colonel, have you ever heard of Einstein's Special Theory of Relativity?"

The Colonel grew white. He knew that no normal teenager could ever know about this concept, especially one who had never

91

begun high school. He knew the history of each of the missing teens. None of them had that kind of background. He hesitated and chose his words carefully. "That means you have been traveling near the speed of light?"

"No sir," said Jose, "Had we traveled that slowly, we would have been dead before we even reached the planet Magma. We actually were traveling far beyond the speed of light. Is that a picture of us, sir?"

Colonel Groundwater had forgotten that he still held the photograph. He regained some composure and quickly showed the photograph to Jose. It was a photograph taken of the group on the day that they all left for their fateful hike up to Mt. Walamalee. The rest of the youth gathered around Jose and started talking about the feelings that they had that day. By their comments Colonel Groundwater was convinced that they were the actual missing youth.

"Can we see our parents, please?" Tykesha pleaded. The others chimed in and gathered around the Colonel.

"Not so fast, kids. First, each one of you have to have a complete medical examination and debriefing session at Bill Air Force Base. A helicopter is being dispatched now to pick us up here." He looked at Sergeant Fargo and snapped his fingers sharply to indicate that he should call for a helicopter. Fargo immediately returned to his jeep and picked up his radio.

The Colonel continued. "Once you have been processed, we will have all of your parents meet you at Bill Air Force Base. Then, you will be free to go to your homes, at least until we need to talk to you again." The teenagers looked at each other, not understanding the full significance of Colonel Groundwater's comment.

The traffic was extremely congested and the Highway Patrol Officers continued to do their best. The cars moved silently and slowly by the group of teenagers and army vehicles. Monica came up to Colonel Groundwater. "Colonel, when we left, cars were a lot different. What happened in the last twenty years to cause them to run so silently and without any smell?"

"They are all run by electric power now. Just after the Winter Olympic Games were over, a severe crisis in the petroleum industry occurred. Major wars among the oil producing countries caused the destruction of the remaining sources of oil. The entire economy of the world was in danger. In order to save the economic basis of the world, everything that once was powered by gasoline, became powered by electricity." Colonel Groundwater excused himself and went to Sergeant Fargo to obtain a report on the arrival of the helicopter. Sergeant Fargo pointed into the air. The Highway Patrol officers had stopped traffic in both directions to allow the helicopter to land in the middle of the freeway. It too ran silently, with only the sound of the blades cutting through the air allowing its arrival to barely be heard.

People had left their cars to watch what was going on. They saw the six teens, an army officer and several other military personnel enter the helicopter. They wondered what the six teenagers had done to be taken by the military. Once the youth were seated, the helicopter lifted silently off the ground and headed over the north Salt Lake area to Bill Air Force Base. Sergeant Fargo returned to his jeep and looking around to make sure that he was alone, changed the frequency on his radio and made a call. He began to speak in a foreign tongue. A reply in the same language came and the communication was complete. He led the caravan back to the outpost.

"Not as smooth as the transporter, but I'd rather be here than there." Maria's comment about the lift off made her friends laugh. A feeling of relief was beginning to fill their minds.

"Transporter?" asked the Colonel. "What's that?"

"It was an interstellar transporter, Colonel Groundwater.," said Steve. "That's what we traveled in. It's kind of like the Cadillac of the space ships. It was developed by a friend of ours and was the first time anyone had ever traveled at the speed of light."

Steve was enjoying the reaction of the Colonel. In his face, he saw a mixture of wonder, disbelief, and then envy of a group of youth who had been the first human beings in recorded history to travel far into the universe beyond the speed of light. Little did the teenagers know the notoriety and danger that awaited them.

The copilot came back and met the six teenagers and told them that their parents had all been notified of their being recovered and that they all were extremely excited. He indicated that they would be allowed to go home with their parents the following evening after being examined at the hospital and by the special officers and investigators from the military and the United States Government. An air of excitement began to be felt around each of the youth. They looked out the windows at the mountains passing under them. They noticed that most had large buildings, probably apartment complexes, built on them. They marveled at the changes that had occurred in only twenty years.

Within fifteen minutes, the helicopter landed on the runway of the air force base near a deserted hanger. Before the youth were allowed to depart, the helicopter went into the hanger and the huge door closed behind it. As they stepped out into the hanger, they were surprised to find a small army of highly armed soldiers. "Why are these soldiers here?" asked Tykesha.

Colonel Groundwater, who heard her comment quickly responded. "They are here to protect you and your friends, Tykesha."

"Why do we need protecting? We're just teenagers." Tykesha looked even more confused. The others gathered around her to listen to the Colonel's answer.

"You're not just ordinary teenagers. You've been missing for twenty years and all of a sudden you appear again and have not aged one year. You tell me about traveling to a planet far into the known universe beyond the speed of light. No, you're not just ordinary teenagers, but will be sought after by the entire world to tell them about the experiences that you've had. I know several foreign governments who would give anything to be in our position now, to learn about the technology that you witnessed during the time you were not on Earth. The only trouble is that those governments are committed to the subjection of the whole free world. If they find out about you, they'll do anything to kidnap you and your friends and use you for their own purposes. We're protecting you against them."

Summer and her friends looked at each other. They silently communicated with their eyes.

We need to call Eclipse now!

They were quickly ushered into the back of a truck that looked

94

somewhat like an armored car. The hanger doors opened and the truck was joined by six other heavily armed vehicles. When they arrived at the hospital, it too was heavily guarded. They were quickly taken to a special examination room. Six doctors were waiting for them.

"Do you have anything on you that was given to you in your journey or is from another planet?" one of the doctors asked the group. Each knew that the communicator and the pack of food that Eclipse had given them were the only items. They were not willing to give away their small green crystals so, to avoid suspicion, they unanimously and silently decided to sacrifice the food.

"The only thing that we have is a one month supply of food that was given to us by our friend." Steve took the pack off of his back and gave it to Colonel Groundwater who quickly accepted it and gave it to two armed men who disappeared with its contents to travel to a laboratory at Bethesda, Maryland.

Satisfied, the physicians took each of the youth into private examination rooms and proceeded to give them a thorough medical checkup. Each of the physicians was completely covered with a large, white suit and white hood with a clear plastic face-plate. They wore surgical gloves. All of this was to prevent them from being contaminated by some incurable disease. At the end of their physical, a phlebotomist came in and took their blood. Her whole body was protected in a similar manner. This made Summer and her friends extremely uncomfortable. Once the blood samples were complete, they were quickly taken to the laboratory to submit them to a variety of chemical and biological tests which included screening for foreign viruses, fungi and bacteria and to determine whether their blood chemistry had been altered during their journey.

The youth were then taken to the hospital cafeteria where they were allowed to eat whatever they wanted. It seemed like a long time since they had tasted fast food, so they ordered hamburgers, fries and a soda. Guards were placed at each door of the cafeteria and anyone entering had to show their identification badge in order to come in. Several soldiers stood around the youth with guns readied.

"I can't live like this," Summer protested in whispers. The

others nodded in agreement. "The first chance each of us gets, we need to call Eclipse and get him here so we can go back to our own time."

Once they had finished their meal, they were all taken to a conference room in the hospital. They sat down and soon were joined by men and women in different kinds of uniforms and some in suits. It was hard for the youth to remember all of their affiliations as they politely introduced themselves: NASA, Secret Service, FBI, Department of the Navy, Air Force and Army were a few that they remembered. Colonel Groundwater was the only familiar face among them. But Summer was looking at one of the men who's face seemed very familiar except for the gray hair on his head that made him look much older. She had remembered him from a picture that her father had and remembered him from his visit to the ridge. Summer took courage and began to speak. "Are you Bill Winter, my father's friend?"

Surprised, the older gentleman said "Yes, how did you recognize me? You and I have never met."

"When you and my father and Doug Volcano came up to the ridge just after we had disappeared into the light, I saw you help my dad look for me and my friends. You didn't have gray hair then."

Dr. Winter smiled but had a puzzled look on his face. "But how could you have seen us. There was nothing up on the mountain at all."

"The transporter that we were in was completely invisible. But all of us were watching you on a large crystalline-like screen in the control room of the transporter." Summer looked at her friends. They remained silent.

"But how did you get into the transporter or..." Doctor Winter paused, "interstellar transporter as Colonel Groundwater has informed us."

Summer was surprised that the Colonel had already shared some of their experiences with this group. She answered his question. "The same way the probe entered; through the red-blue side of the light. This light was caused by the presence of static electricity from the severe lightning." Summer stopped talking to allow what she had said to be understood by her listeners. Doctor

96

Winter was impressed by the tremendous knowledge Summer had gained.

An old VCR machine and television were brought into the conference room. Video had been completely digitized onto small compact discs, and the old VCR machines were almost like antiques. The tape taken by the probe was played to the group that was present. It was the first time that the tape had been shown to all agencies of the government since the teenagers' disappearance. The adults were visibly shaken by the appearance of the monster. The youth became "homesick" as they saw Eclipse. Another investigator from NASA asked them to explain why the creature who destroyed the probe didn't kill them.

Summer and her friends then took turns telling them the entire story of their friend Eclipse, the things that they learned in the computer programs of the space ship, the purpose of their journey, the potential danger to Earth's biomes, and their experience on the planet Magma. They also talked about the universe and their feelings when they saw the earth disappear as they left the solar system. They talked about how Einstein's Special Theory of Relativity related to their lack of aging and how Eclipse was to come back to return them to their own time. It was well past midnight when the youth completed their story. They were extremely tired and were shown to a portion of the hospital that had been completely cleared for their stay. They went to bed and slept the entire night, under heavy security.

The group continued meeting well into the early hours of the morning. Some doubted the youths' story and thought that it might be made up. But the overwhelming fact of the lack of aging of the teenagers was the only thing that brought the reality of their experience to a general acceptance by the whole group.

"We can't afford to let these youth go back in time, if it really is possible to go back in time." Colonel Groundwater cautioned.

"Of course it's possible, Colonel," Doctor Winter affirmed. "How else could the youth have traveled so far and return in such a short time from the time they left. Einstein's theory states that at near the speed of light, that a ten year journey, a mere fraction of how far they actually said they traveled, would result in a seventy year difference of time, not a twenty year difference."

A three-star general from the Air Force spoke authoritatively. "Rather than preventing them from going back, let's try convincing the youth to allow us to talk to this friend of theirs and learn directly from him about the source of power of his transporter and the secrets of super light travel. Then let them go back if they want."

The suggestion was adopted and a telephone call made to the White House to inform the President of the progress made and the results of their decision. They then left to get some breakfast.

The next morning, Summer and her friends were separated the whole day and individually interviewed and questioned about the details of their experiences. Their stories coincided exactly, except for their individual adventures in the biomes where Eclipse had assigned them. Thus the conclusion of the report was that they had undergone a real experience. Including breakfast and lunch, the interviews lasted until three o'clock in the afternoon when the families began to arrive to pick up their children. The six were brought together just prior to the time they were to meet their parents. A representative of the President of the United States was there to talk to them. He told them of the President's gratefulness that they were all right and hoped that they realized how important their experiences would be for the benefit of all mankind. He urged them not to talk to anyone that they did not know very well about their journey. He asked that in those situations where they did talk, that they would limit what they told others to a description of what happened to them and how they felt about the events that transpired during their trip. The youth reluctantly agreed, shook the representative's hand, and went to meet their parents.

Excitement filled the room as the six teenagers ran toward their families. They had all significantly aged, partly because of the years that had gone by, but mostly because of the worry of losing their children. The final acceptance that they were gone forever also caused their parents to age rapidly. They ran and embraced each other, tears of joy flowing freely. After minutes of excited talking, weeping and more talking, their parents stepped aside as a group of young men and young women in their twenties and thirties came into the room. Some had little children of their own. It took a little while for each to recognize their younger brothers and sisters- wait-now their older brothers and sisters. It all seemed so strange.

In spite of seeing their younger brothers and sisters as adults, they ran and hugged them and cried some more. Finally, it was time for them to separate and to return to their own homes. Two secret service agents were assigned to each of the teenagers to protect them twenty-four hours a day. The agents followed each family to their respective homes. The six youth groaned about the lack of privacy and longed for the time when they were just insignificant teenagers.

Even with the lack of privacy, Summer was happy being at home. She didn't like how her mother, father, two sisters and brother had aged. Her dad, she found out, was in his last year of high school teaching before retirement. Her mother had experienced a bout with cancer which had been in remission for over ten years. It felt so strange that in the short time that they were gone, not more than ten days by their calculations, that over twenty years had already passed on Earth. Then Summer felt lucky to see her parents at all, realizing that, had it not been for Eclipse who took them back into time that she could have come back to Earth during a time when the great, great, great, great grandchildren of her sisters and brother were adults.

"I have a surprise for you Summer," Tom Solstice said as they drove up in front of their home. Because it had been recently painted it looked just like the day when Summer had left, except that the trees were much bigger.

"Please tell me the surprise, Dad." The three entered the home. One of the agents stayed outside and the other came inside with them.

"Do you have to be with me all of the time?" Summer asked the female agent, trying not to be rude but not doing a very good job at it.

"Yes, that's what we were told to do. Someone will also sit in your room as you sleep each night."

Summer mumbled under her breath. "Oh great! I have to be treated like a..."

To save the agent further embarrassment, Tom Solstice interrupted his daughter. "I want you to meet our new science teacher tomorrow. He has taken Mr. Quake's place who retired last year. Tomorrow is Friday and he would like you to come and talk to all of his Earth Science and Astronomy classes."

"Is that the surprise?"

"Not exactly, Summer, but when you see the new science teacher, you will understand what the surprise is to be."

"Will Jose, Steve, Tykesha, Mon..."

"Yes, Summer," Mr. Solstice interrupted. "The surprise involves you and your friends."

Between the attention that her parents gave her and the continual presence of the Secret Service agents, she wasn't able to communicate with Eclipse for the rest of the day. With the agent right outside the door, she couldn't even use the communicator in the bathroom because, in order to speak loud enough for Eclipse to hear, the agent would overhear also. She assumed that her friends were having the same problem.

Summer woke up several times that night in the hopes of calling Eclipse. Each time, the female agent was in her room. Summer finally gave up and slept the rest of the night.

The anticipation of the day caused Summer to get up very early. She went outside into the back yard and walked around the entire yard, remembering the fun that she used to have with her younger brother and sisters as they played hide and seek, croquette and had water fights during the summertime. She felt cheated that this experience had suddenly been taken from her.

"Summer, come in for breakfast" Summer looked at the smiling face of her aging mother and smiled at her. "I'll be right there, Mom."

Mr. Solstice entered the kitchen at the same time as Summer. He hugged her and then pinched himself. "What did you do that for, Dad?"

"I just can't believe that this is real. I want it to continue, forever." He hugged his daughter again. Mrs. Solstice called them to sit down to eat. The two special agents had already eaten and were preparing for the busy day ahead.

After breakfast, Summer and her father left home for the short two-mile drive to the high school, closely followed by the Secret

Service agents. After parking in the teachers' lot, Summer and her father walked into the school with the Secret Service agents walking on either side. She could see Steve and Tykesha waiting for her by the door. She burst into a sprint and joined them within seconds. The agents looked all around nervously and ran behind her. Shortly, Jose, Monica and Maria arrived, closely followed by their Secret Service agents.

They walked in a tight group down the school hallway. Students stared at the official-looking group of men and women agents who walked with them on every side. Entering Mr. Solstice's classroom, all, except the agents, sat down. They looked and saw computers around the outside wall of the entire classroom. Large benches and television monitors with interactive, multimedia computers near the benches filled the center of the room. Summer realized that it was completely different than the way the classroom had been arranged twenty years ago. She had visited her father's classroom often. Mr. Solstice put down the papers he had brought from home and quickly readied the room for his own students. He then faced Summer, her friends and the twelve agents. "The new science teacher will be here in about two minutes. After I introduce him, you will follow him to his classroom. School starts in fifteen minutes."

Three minutes had passed and the six teenagers were impatient to find out the surprise that had been promised. The door finally opened. Their eyes opened wide and their mouths dropped nearly to the floor. It was Doug Volcano.

"You're the science teacher?" Steve asked spontaneously in disbelief. Doug smiled and nodded affirmatively. He had changed since they had last seen him. He was now thirty seven years old- old enough to be their own father. He had gained a pot-belly from the good cooking of his wife and he was slightly bald on top of his head. The six youth spontaneously jumped from their seats and crowded around him.

When a moment of silence came he looked at them and spoke. "Ever since the day I took the five of you to the mountains, I have felt horrible at being the one to cause you to disappear. I have never forgiven myself for that. You can imagine how grateful I was to hear that you had returned." The first bell rang and the entire group walked the short distance to Mr. Volcano's classroom.

When they entered, they noticed six chairs neatly set in front of the room. "Those are for you," Doug said with a big smile. They quickly sat down, noticing that Doug's room was similar to Mr. Solstice's room, except for the presence of the gas jets, Bunsen burners, beakers, flasks and the sinks, denoting a science laboratory. Two agents entered the room and the remaining ten stationed themselves outside of the window of the classroom. Others took their position in the hallway outside the door of the classroom.

Students were entering the room quickly now since the tardy bell was about to ring. They sensed something special as they saw six of their peers sitting in front of their room. Students sat quickly at their assigned work-stations. Mr. Volcano punched several keys on the computer keyboard on his desk. Then he came and stood in front of Summer and her friends and began speaking to the class. "Now that roll is taken, I want to introduce you to the six individuals sitting behind me. At first, you will not believe what I tell you, but after they talk to you, you will realize that the experience we are about to tell you is true. Twenty-one years ago, I was only three years older than these six teenagers. They were fourteen then and they are fourteen now."

Noise quickly exploded from different parts of the room as members of his class gasped and spoke to their neighbors in amazement. He continued and they listened intently. "Now, I am twenty-three years older than they. For the past two weeks of their life and twenty-one years of my life, they have had an adventure in the farthest realms of the universe."

Another wave of whispering and gasps of shock occurred among his students. Then Mr. Volcano introduced the six and told how he had taken five of them to locate Summer after she had disappeared. He described what happened to them and how badly he had felt about what he had done. Then all eyes were riveted on the six teenagers as they began their story. While Steve was speaking about arriving on the planet Magma, an idea suddenly came to Summer. She waited for the appropriate moment and then pulled on his shirt. He paused and looked at her and she silently made him understand that she wanted to speak now. He stopped and

102

let her begin. "Before we left to our individual biomes, Eclipse, who was the name of our friend, gave each of us a piece of green glass, something like this one that I found at home."

Summer pulled out her communicator and showed it to the class. Her friends knew exactly what she was doing. "He explained to us that all we had to do was to call the person by name and our communicators would automatically connect to that communicator. Let's pretend that I was in trouble and wanted to communicate with Eclipse. Let me show you how I would do it."

She brought the communicator close to her mouth, watching carefully for any response from the agents in the room. You could hear a pin drop in the classroom. "Eclipse, this is Summer. We're on Earth in the year two thousand sixteen and we need your help. Thank you." She noticed that the agents in the room had gained a great deal of interest in the communicator at that very moment, so she put it back into her pocket and continued speaking.

"We all wish that Eclipse hadn't taken our communicators. We miss our friend and would like some day to talk to him again." She noticed that the agents had relaxed. "Now, Tykesha will finish our story."

When the bell had rung after ninety minutes, the class sat in complete shock because of the story that they had just heard. Some thought this was one of Mr. Volcano's jokes and a clever way to teach them about the universe, suns and solar systems. But because of the surrounding adults in suits and ties, they figured that this was for real. After realizing that the period was actually over, they got up and surrounded the youth and started to ask them questions. Summer had to go to the bathroom and leaned over to Tykesha and told her where she was going. Several other students were leaving at about the same time and so she left with them. Because she blended in so well, the Secret Service agents did not notice when she left. By the time they discovered that she wasn't in the room, Summer was already in the bathroom.

The two agents in the room walked quickly to the five youth and interrupted their conversation with Mr. Volcano's students. "Where did Summer go?" they asked tensely.

"To the bathroom," Tykesha responded. "She'll be okay."

The agents didn't listen to this comment but bolted out of the classroom, almost hitting some students walking by the doorway. They stopped momentarily to ask them where the girl's bathroom was.

"Around that corner and to the end of the hall" was the reply.

They quickly rounded the corner and saw the bathroom door open. Out came Summer. The agents stopped and relaxed, knowing that she was all right. They turned around for a moment, and as they did, Summer screamed. They turned around quickly in time to see two men, who had entered through an outside door at the end of the hall, grab Summer, place a pillow case over her head and begin to drag her toward the door. They drew their weapons and yelled at the men to stop. Instead, one produced an automatic weapon and aimed it at the two agents rapidly firing several shots. Students in the hallways screamed and dropped to the floor as the two Secret Service agents fell wounded, unable to continue pursuit. They radioed for backup. The agents stationed outside saw the men drag Summer out of the door. A delivery truck was parked right outside with the back door opened. Before they could respond, the two men and Summer disappeared into the back of the delivery truck, the back door closed and the truck sped away. The agents radioed for help and gave a description of the delivery truck as they ran for their cars.

The truck traveled quickly to an abandoned field less than a mile away where a helicopter was waiting. The driver and the two men in the back forced Summer into the hands of two men who waited inside the helicopter. It lifted off the ground and headed for the mountains at the east side of the valley. Each of the men who stayed behind placed a capsule inside their mouths and swallowed it.

Within minutes, police and Secret Service cars converged on the delivery truck. They had seen the helicopter take off only moments earlier. Scrambling out of their cars with revolvers drawn, they found three men laying on the ground, dead. The agents searched the horizon in the direction that they had seen the helicopter take off. They easily located it. One of the agents ran to his car and radioed the current position of the helicopter to all agencies and requested help with the three bodies they had discovered.

Summer's captors continued heading east. The helicopter passed through turbulent air as they flew over the first mountain range. Summer had been gagged in the delivery truck and her hands tied behind her back. The pillowcase still covered her face. As she was placed aboard the helicopter, she was squeezed into a small space on the floor behind the pilot. The space was so small, she couldn't move. She felt like she couldn't get enough air and began to groan, trying to communicate her condition to the men.

"Make no noise!" one of the men diabolically growled in a thick accent. She ignored him and continued moaning loudly. The man who had warned her, hit her solidly on the cheek with the back of his hand. Summer lay still, afraid to move or make a noise.

The helicopter dipped low into the sky to avoid detection by radar devices and skimmed the tops of the trees of the first set of mountains. When the tops of a second set of mountains were cleared, the man who had hit Summer pointed to a small valley in the distance and talked to the pilot in a foreign language. The pilot turned toward a deserted clearing with an old dirt airstrip that once was used by executives of a logging company. There, a two engine private airplane waited, ready to take off immediately upon transfer of the girl. The helicopter landed twenty-five yards from the airplane. The two men pulled Summer out of the helicopter, carried her to the private plane and delivered her into the arms of a large man with thick black eyebrows. Effortlessly, he climbed into the airplane, closed the outside door and gently deposited Summer on a small, but comfortable seat and placed a seat belt around her. She was so weak from her ordeal in the truck and helicopter that she collapsed into a deep sleep. The man entered the cockpit and sat down by the pilot who was stroking his thick, black beard. The two men looked out of the cockpit and watched the helicopter take off. Then, the pilot rapidly increased the throttle to make sure they could take off on the short runway. The electricity-driven engines quickly increased in power and the airplane's brakes were released. As they cleared the tops of the trees surrounding the clearing, the man who had carried Summer aboard took out a strange-looking miniature box and pushed a button. Instantaneously the helicopter, now two miles distant, exploded and vaporized into small pieces of plastic and metal.

The entire school was in commotion. Summer's friends were horrified and sat, dazed, with tears streaming from their eyes. Students in the hallway were crying and talking to each other about the gun battle they had witnessed, the wounding of the men in suits and the kidnapping of a girl they didn't know. Mr. Volcano's students became distraught and disoriented. He attempted to help his class, but his own feelings of sorrow prevented him from being successful. The Secret Service agents of the remaining five youth walked into Mr. Volcano's room and stood in front of Summer's friends. Monica looked up.

"It's time for all of you to go with us," one of the agents said authoritatively. "You all will have to go back with us to Bill Air Force Base immediately so that you can be more adequately protected. We have received word that all of your lives might be in danger."

"But what about our families? We've just had less than a day with them!" Jose protested.

The agents did not respond but stood and glared at the youth until they finally stood up. The ten agents circled the youth and led them toward five government cars that were awaiting them in the school parking lot. Surrounding the cars were at least fifteen heavily armed jeeps and a few armored cars that looked like modified tanks. Each youth and their agents got into one of the five cars and the caravan slowly moved out of the parking lot. All of the students in the school, as well as the teachers and administrators, followed them out and stared at the sight, unable to believe what had just transpired to the six "time travelers" at their school. The news of the experience of Summer and her friends quickly spread throughout the entire student body. All knew of their experiences by the time the caravan disappeared.

State Police cars and motorcycles were at the front and the rear of the caravan, with their emergency lights flashing, leading the caravan without stopping at the major intersections of the city. When they reached the interstate, the progress was more rapid.

106

Sirens were turned on and the entire group of vehicles proceeded swiftly without hindrance, passing hundreds of cars of curious onlookers staring in bewilderment at the unusual sight. Many thought that the President of the United States sat in one of the cars. Others felt that there was some local emergency. They looked around for smoke or some sign which might give them a clue.

The caravan passed, without stopping, through the main gate of Bill Air Force Base and turned toward a small row of barracks that had been reserved by the base commander to protect the five youth. Amidst protests by Summer's friends, they were escorted under heavy guard into the barracks. Each was assigned a separate room and told to stay inside their rooms until further notice.

"This sounds like some kind of illegal detention to me," Steve boomed. His comment was met by stern looks from the military around him. For a moment, Steve thought that they might hit him, so he quietly submitted to their request and entered his room. Once inside, armed guards were placed all along the entire hallway and around the barracks, as well as in their rooms. All of the entrances to Bill Air Force Base were manned with armored vehicles and men with powerful weapons.

CHAPTER 8

Summer was awakened suddenly and felt like she was smothering to death. She began to moan loudly, trying to get someone to remove the pillowcase from her head. Hearing footsteps coming toward her, she winced, expecting to be slapped once again. Instead, for the first time since she had been kidnapped, the pillowcase and gag were removed. She breathed in deep gulps of air. The sunshine entering the airplane window shined into Summer's face and blinded her for a moment. She quickly shut her eyes and then opened them carefully. As they adapted to the bright sunshine, she could make out the form of a young woman. She blinked several times.

The young woman had coal-black hair, much like Summer's. She sat down on the seat opposite Summer and smiled. "Hello, my name is Eli. Welcome to my country," she said in a thick accent.

Summer felt disoriented. "Where are we? How long have I been here?"

"Since you were taken from your high school, it has been two days. You are now on a private jet and we are about one hour from landing in the capital of my country. We have been flying for the last six hours."

"What's the name of your country?"

"Iraq."

Summer stared at the pretty young woman for a moment. "How long have I been asleep.. or was I unconscious?"

"Ever since you left the helicopter about eighteen hours ago. After the helicopter, a small airplane brought you to this jet. You must be thirsty and hungry." Summer nodded weakly and tried to wet her lips with her tongue, but her mouth felt like dry cotton. "I will bring you something to give you strength and help your thirst."

She disappeared into the front of the small jet. Summer looked out of the window and saw a large sea below them. They were flying parallel to the shoreline of a landmass that she didn't recognize. It looked like there was a lot of sand in the interior of the country. From the position of the sun, she knew that she was looking at the northern part of the country. Hmmm, could this be the northern part of Africa, she thought to herself.

The young woman interrupted Summer's thoughts as she brought back a tray of food. "The Mediterranean Sea is very blue this time of year, isn't it?"

Summer looked up and tried to manage a smile and nodded in response to her question. "Yes, it's very beautiful." So she _was_ right after all. They _were_ heading toward the East... toward Iraq and the sandy area to the south _was_ Africa! She looked toward the front of the small jet and, in the distance, could barely detect another large mass of land where the Mediterranean Sea ended.

"Here is some soda and a dinner for you." Eli placed the tray on the opposite seat and then untied the cords that held Summer's arms and hands. She then gave the tray to Summer. Thanking Eli for her kindness, Summer began gulping down her food and soda.

"Don't eat too fast. You may become ill." Eli gently touched Summer's shoulder.

Summer relaxed and slowed down. After she took her next bite of food, she looked up at the young woman. "Eli, why have I been kidnapped and treated so badly?...except for you of course."

A moment of silence followed as the young woman looked down, avoiding Summer's piercing glance. "I am very sorry for the way that our people have treated you. You are here to meet an important government official of my country but I have not been told what will take place in your meeting or even why you have been brought here. If you are willing to tell me, I would be very interested to listen."

"It's too long of a story to tell right now." Eli seemed sincere and genuinely concerned about her welfare, but Summer was not sure whether she should trust her and decided to say nothing. Nonetheless, Summer was grateful for at least one friendly face. The young woman sat quietly and watched as Summer completed her meal, wondering what secret Summer held within her. When Summer was done, Eli removed the tray and returned it to the front of the jet. As soon as she disappeared Summer reached quickly into the pockets of her jeans. She breathed a sigh of relief as she felt the communicator in her left pocket. She was about to remove it when

Eli returned.

"Fasten your seat belt. We will be landing in twenty-five minutes. There will be much air turbulence as we approach Baghdad. From Baghdad, you will be taken blindfolded, but not tied or gagged, to the place of your meeting." She sat down in the seat opposite Summer and fastened her seat belt. After Summer had complied with the request, she watched the ground come closer and closer as the jet approached the International Airport at Baghdad.

The limousine turned onto a side road. The pavement ended and the road began to twist and turn as it approached some little hills outside of Baghdad. The road gradually got smaller until it was wide enough for only one car. After several more turns, the limousine stopped as the road stopped, directly against the side of a hill. Suddenly, part of the hill in front of the car began to move to one side, revealing a continuation of the road inside. The limousine entered and the opening began to close behind it. After only fifty yards, the limousine stopped. Even with the blindfold completely covering her eyes, Summer could tell that they had entered into a place with decreased light. She was escorted out of the limousine and into another series of doors and passageways that went deeper underground. After a short walk, a trip on an elevator and walking down one flight of stairs, they entered the office of the Minister of Defense of Iraq.

Summer felt afraid as the blindfold was removed from her eyes. She was standing in front of a large, oval desk of what appeared to be a secretary who was talking to the man who had brought her from the airport. They talked in the same strange language she had heard when she first was kidnapped. Finally, the secretary got up and showed Summer through a door and into a spacious office with no windows. A large man with a bushy, straight mustache, a military uniform and thin, gray-black hair sat behind the desk. He looked up as the door opened and, when he saw that it was Summer, quickly stood and walked toward her. The secretary saluted and then turned and left the room, closing the door behind him.

"Welcome, Summer Solstice. I am Amir Kasafuut. I trust that the last part of your journey was more peaceful than the first?" Amir forced a smile which did not significantly change a stern, ruthless expression.

Summer nodded, nervously. Looking around the room, she said, "why aren't there any windows here or in your secretary's office?"

"We are under the ground, Summer."

"Why have you kidnapped me and brought me to Iraq?" Summer noticed that he spoke with almost no accent at all.

"We need your help and knew that your government would not allow us the privilege of meeting you and finding out what happened to you during the last twenty-one earth years since you disappeared." He watched her as he spoke. He was very impressed by the fact that she hadn't aged during all of those years. In fact, if he had not seen her with his own eyes, he would have never believed that such a thing was possible.

"You haven't brought me here just for me to tell you the story of our trip, have you," Summer said, looking at him coolly.

"I can tell that you like directness. This is good. We will get along very well. We need the secret of the power of the space ship that you traveled in. The nation that obtains and uses this power source will govern the world. I am sure that you have noticed that the oil resources of the earth have all but disappeared and probably know that electricity is not an efficient source of energy to power our vehicles and airplanes,"

"But I don't know the secret of his transporter. He never shared it with us...and we never asked him."

Amir raised his eyebrows when he heard the word, "transporter". "I know that. But the alien that brought you back to earth brought you back over twenty years beyond the time he should have. I believe that he meant to bring you back to your own time and when he learns of his mistake, will be back for you. Am I correct?"

Summer refused to answer but looked away from him. Amir looked at her for a minute, then smiled and grunted. "I thought so. How were you going to call him?"

Again there was silence. "Summer, we are prepared to have you stay with us until we have an opportunity to speak with this alien. You could be here for the rest of your life and never see your family again."

112

Summer cringed at the thought of being held captive in a foreign country. She couldn't stand to live the rest of her life in Iraq. "Okay, he gave us a communicator to call him and he told us.." Summer suddenly stopped. It occurred to her that all electromagnetic waves travel at the speed of light. She remembered Eclipse saying that his planet was many millions of light years away from earth. Her heart sank. The communication that she had made before she was kidnapped might take millions of years to get to Eclipse. Eclipse might not be alive by then. Certainly, she would be dead by the time he received the message. She felt weak and looked for the nearest chair and sat down, almost passing out.

"What is the matter Summer? Are you all right?"

Summer looked up at Amir. She noticed that he had several medals hanging on his left pocket. "I think I'm just tired from the trip."

"But of course, how insensitive of me. A room is prepared for you down the hall. Would you like to rest for a while before continuing our little discussion?"

"I think I'm okay Mr. Amir. I'd rather get this done, if it's all the same to you." Amir nodded approval and sat down beside her. He pressed the "record" button of a cassette tape player that he had on the table near where Summer was sitting. Summer looked at the recorder suspiciously and hesitated for a second. Then she began, her mind racing wildly.

"Let's see, where was I. Oh yes... our friend gave us a small gray, metallic-like communicator to call him if we needed him." Summer knew that she had to lie about the looks of the communicator so that the real communicator would remain safe in her pocket. "Because I was kidnapped by your men, I wasn't able to call our friend to come back and take us back to the time when we first left with him. Even if I could, there's two small problems."

Amir frowned. "What are they?"

"Well, Eclipse... that's our friend's name... didn't tell us how the communicator worked. If it works on the basis of current earth communicators, then the message I would send would take millions of years to get there, based on travelling only at the speed of light."

"That means that we will all be dead when he gets the

113

message," Amir responded with dismay. Then he became thoughtful, and a glimmer of anger and then satisfaction crossed his face. "Surely your friend, Eclipse would not have given you a communicator which would never allow you to reach him in your lifetime."

Summer hoped that he was right, because she was not happy with the idea of living in Iraq for the rest of her life and dying without ever seeing her parents again.

"What is the other problem you speak of, Summer?"

"Sometime during the kidnapping, my communicator was lost, so I have no way to call Eclipse."

Amir cursed. He sat there for a minute, deep in thought and then looked at Summer. "Do your friends have communicators with them?"

"I believe that they have only one communicator." Summer knew that each had one small, green crystal communicator device.

Amir smiled diabolically as a plan for the acquisition of the communicator came to him. He looked at Summer and then into the air and smiled again. Summer became uneasy. "I will want to see you in the morning. We have one more thing to take care of in order to obtain another communicator. Go and get some food and rest." He pushed a button and his secretary appeared in the doorway. He requested that Summer be taken to her quarters and he immediately obeyed.

The telephone rang in the office of the President of the United States. His secretary answered and quickly tensed as the caller began talking. President Ohm came out of his office and was about to leave when he saw his secretary frantically signaling him to wait and get ready to answer the telephone. "Yes sir," she said into the telephone. "The President will have to talk to you directly on this matter."

President Ohm quickly returned to the oval office, closing the door behind him. He was concerned about the worried look of his veteran secretary of fifteen years. He walked quickly to his desk, sat down, waiting for her to connect him to the mysterious caller. The intercom buzzed and President Ohm pushed line one and lifted the receiver. "Yes, who is this?"

"Mr. President, this is General Amir Kasafuut."

"Why am I not talking to your chief, Amir."

"He is fully aware of my communication with you and supports it fully."

"What do you want, Amir? This is a little late for you to be at work, isn't it?"

Amir did not like the subtle joke. It was only six o'clock at night, an hour that he usually left his office. He used every bit of his self-control to avoid insulting the President of the United States. "I would like to invite you and the five youth that you are guarding in Utah to tune to the CNV International News Channel in exactly twelve hours from now."

"And if I don't, Amir?"

"Then Summer Solstice will die."

President Ohm stood up quickly, anger flashing in his eyes. "So it was you who kidnapped the girl!"

"Of course." Amir said proudly. "Right under the very noses of your top agents." He paused for a moment and then began again in a sinister tone. "Mr. President, I will know if you and Summer's five friends do not watch the program tonight."

"Let me talk to Summer!" President Ohm demanded. There was no response-- only silence on the other end of the line.

"Watch the television tonight," Amir repeated and he hung up the telephone.

"Sarah!" bellowed the President. His secretary raced into the oval office. "Call General Lever at Bill Air Force Base. I want to talk to him now!"

"It's only six o'clock in the morning there, Mr. President."

"I know! Do it!" She quickly left the office and within a minute had awaken the General in his home.

"Good morning, Mr.President. What's the emergency?" General Lever yawned as he spoke.

"Iraq has Summer Solstice. They are threatening to kill her if we don't allow her five friends to watch a special on the CNV network tonight at six o'clock your time." There was silence on the other end of the telephone. "Lever, are you there?"

"Yes sir, Mr.President. I'm shocked. What do you suppose is

going to happen?"

"I haven't the slightest idea, General. In twelve hours, the whole world will know."

It was almost six o'clock at night when the five youths were escorted into another area of their barracks. The number of men had been doubled after the call from the President that morning. Summer's friends had been wondering about the reasons for the increased protection they were receiving. They felt like they were being held hostage. Soldiers were in each of their rooms during the entire night and did not leave them alone, except to go to the bathroom. Even then, they stood by the bathroom door and outside of the bathroom windows. The youth felt angry as they were told to sit down on the couch to watch the television.

"Why do we have to do that?" Jose said belligerently, refusing to sit down. "Why are we prisoners here in our own state and country?"

The soldiers looked at Jose unsympathetically and repeated the order. He remained standing. Three soldiers moved toward him and were about to lay their hands on his arms to physically enforce the order, when he decided that he had better sit down with his four friends.

General Lever entered the room and walked up to the television and turned on the power. He flipped the channels with the remote until CNV International was selected. The youth recognized him from their original interrogation when they had just arrived back to the earth. He hadn't said much during the entire questioning period.

"Oh great, we're forced to sit here to watch some stupid news show with the General," Tykesha whispered to Monica and Maria. The General came and sat down by the youth and they became quiet, curious about the secrecy of this strange event.

Just then the news announcer began. "We interrupt our normal programming to bring you a special interview from outside of Baghdad, Iraq. We take you to our correspondent who is in the office of the Minister of Defense of Iraq."

"In a historical announcement, Iraq has requested CNV to broadcast a special interview with General Amir Kasafuut and a young woman who is visiting him from the United States."

116

Summer's five friends suddenly took interest in the news program. Could it be Summer?

The picture faded to two individuals.

"Summer!" Tykesha and Monica screamed in unison. Maria and Jose gasped audibly.

"Summer's in Iraq?" Steve breathed in disbelief.

"Be quiet!" General Lever responded. "We need to hear the content of this interview."

General Kasafuut had just introduced Summer as a special guest of Iraq and as a young woman who has been fourteen years old for the last twenty-one earth years. The CNV Baghdad correspondent challenged the Minister of Defense as to the truthfulness of his statement.

"You must ask Miss Solstice. She has five friends who together have been traveling through the universe at well beyond the speed of light for only a short period of time. During that time, her age did not change while we aged twenty-one years. They are watching at this very moment in a barracks on Bill Air Force Base in the United States."

The camera zoomed in on Summer's face. "She looks scared," Maria said, empathizing with the feelings of her friend.

"Miss Solstice, what have you to say with the General's statement about your activities during the last twenty-one years?"

"It's true. We have been to a new planet in an uncharted galaxy of our universe. But I have no idea if my friends are watching."

Almost laughing in disbelief, the correspondent interrupted. "And what were you doing at that planet?"

"We were collecting, plants, insects, animals and soil samples that have become extinct on the planet of the man who took us. His planet is dying because his people have misused their resources and he wanted to bring back all that stuff to his planet to save it."

The correspondent found himself without words. Amir took advantage of the break to initiate his plan. "The friend she talks about, Eclipse is his name...." Amir paused for effect.

"How did he find all that stuff out?" Monica said, worried about what was happening to Summer. She could picture Summer being brainwashed and tortured. General Lever looked at Monica sternly.

Amir continued. "....was to have brought Summer and her friends back to earth twenty-one years ago, but because of a miscalculation, returned them to our time instead." Amir paused, and when no one interrupted him, he continued. "Summer has a small problem. She and her friends have been given two metallic communicators to call their friend so that he can return to earth and take them back to their own time. She has not yet called him and, in her journey to Iraq, has lost her communicator."

Tykesha and her friends looked at each other strangely. They knew that Summer had called Eclipse just before she was kidnapped. They also knew that the communicators were small green crystals and that each of them had one in their pockets. She obviously had not told Amir all of the truth during her brainwashing sessions. Was the fact that she had lost her communicator a lie also?

"She needs the other communicator that one of the five youth at Bill Air Force Base has. One of my men is within a hundred yards of the main gate of Bill Air Force Base, waiting to escort one of the youth and the communicator to Iraq immediately. I would ask that General Lever, the commander of the base, send one of Summer's friends with the communicator so that she can call Eclipse. When he comes, then all on our earth will see, for the first time, a space ship that travels beyond the speed of light and a life form from another galaxy."

CNV news crews were immediately dispatched to Bill Air Force Base from their regional office in Salt Lake City. The correspondent continued asking another question to General Kasafuut.

As General Kasafuut was answering, General Lever looked angrily at the five youth. "Which one of you has been hiding the communicator. I want to know now!"

"None of us have any small metallic device," Steve said truthfully. "Eclipse never gave us anything like that. Summer's trying to give us a message. For some reason, she needs one of us to come to her now."

That comment caused the General to think seriously about capitalizing on this situation to send a team into the heart of Iraq to free the girl.

"I have one request for General Lever before we end this interview." The correspondent nodded his head for Kasafuut to continue. The cameras were focused on the Minister of Defense. General Lever was now listening carefully. "General, you are only to send one of the youth. If someone comes with the youth or follows, or if no one comes, Summer Solstice shall die."

The network suddenly cut the transmission and returned to the New York center. "CNV is not responsible for the contents of its interviews and apologizes to the family and friends of Summer Solstice for this barbaric falsification of an interview. CNV teams are about to arrive at Bill Air Force Base in order to confirm or deny the story you have just heard. We will take you live to Bill Air Force Base in just a few minutes. Meanwhile, elsewhere in the news the drought in Africa has continued in the south of the continent for......"

An aide quickly walked into the barracks room and stepped briskly up to General Lever and saluted. "Sir, a Mr. Solstice has called the base, wanting to speak to you. He has seen the interview on CNV. Also, three CNV trucks have just arrived at the main gate. News teams are demanding entrance to the base to see you." The General looked at the television and saw the picture change to the main gate of Bill Air Force Base. Now, the whole world was watching what would happen on his front porch.

Lever knew he had to make a decision quickly. Before he had time to think, another aide quickly came into the room with a red cellular telephone in her hand. "General, Sir. The President of the United States wishes to speak with you immediately." She handed him the cellular telephone. There hadn't been that much excitement at the base for twenty-one years, ever since Summer and her friends had disappeared.

General Lever took the telephone and slowly put it to his ear. "Yes sir, Mr. President?"

"What on earth is happening there, Lever!" the President yelled. "Look at the television!"

As General Lever looked at the screen his mouth opened wide in horror. A man at the gate was just introducing himself as General Amir Kasafuut's aide who had come to pick up one of Summer

119

Solstice's friends from the base.

Lever still was unable to respond. "What are we going to do about this General?" the President continued yelling. "My Chief of Staff says that we must lie and tell the press that there are no youth there. If we ever admitted that we have been covering this situation up for twenty-one years, then all hell will break loose."

"I'm with the youth now, Mr. President. I concur with the Chief of Staff's decision, unless you want me to do something else."

"No Lever. We have no other choice."

"What about Summer?" The General talked softer so that the five youth standing near wouldn't hear him.

"She's expendable." The President terminated the transmission and looked at the floor in deep thought.

General Lever handed the telephone back to his aide and then looked at the other aide and said, "Tell Mr. Solstice that I will be back with him as soon as I handle the problem at the gate." Both aides saluted him and returned to their duties. He looked at the commander of the security detachment. "Colonel, I want these youth returned to their quarters immediately with no contact with the outside world. They are to eat in their rooms."

"But General Lever," Steve protested. "Summer needs our help! You heard Amir. She'll be killed if one of us doesn't come!" Steve was yelling loudly now. The General ignored him and walked out of the barracks, heading to the main gate. The Colonel ordered his men to return the youth to their rooms. The men formed around the youth and escorted them out of the television room. As they left the area Steve saw an open door to his right. Without thinking he bolted out of the door, trying to remember how to get to the main gate. Maybe he could tell the true story to CNV reporters. His movement was so rapid that he knocked down one of the soldiers. It took the others several seconds to respond. Two ran out of the door behind Steve and the Colonel followed them. The others remained behind to guard the four frightened teenagers.

Steve was already forty yards away from them. One of the men stopped and put his rifle to his shoulder. He aimed to the right of Steve's feet and fired once. Steve heard the crack of a gun behind him and saw the bullet hit the powdery soil to his right. He jumped in fear but began to run even faster.

Wound him in the leg!" the Colonel ordered.

"The rifleman readied his weapon, aiming at the top of his left leg. The cross hairs found their mark and he squeezed the trigger. The bullet tore Steve's pants and grazed his leg. The pain caused him to trip and fall. He rolled down a small hill in front of him, stopping at the edge of a mountain stream that meandered through the base. Steve held his leg in pain. He looked down and saw his pants torn with his blood wetting the material. He quickly examined his wound and realized that the bullet did not enter his leg. Breathing a momentary sigh of relief, he began to look around to see if there was somewhere to hide. The sound of the soldiers feet pounding the earth, pursuing him, could now be clearly heard. Any moment, they would appear over the top of the little hill and would see him. If they caught him he was sure that they would do something horrible.

Steve saw a small pond area out of the corner of his eye. He turned and looked. It was almost completely hidden by a thick grove of pine trees. He hoped that the water would be deep enough. Without thinking he dragged himself into the cold mountain water and crawled as fast as he could toward the secluded pond. The sun was close to setting in the western sky. The shadows of the trees covered the stream and pond area.

When the four youth heard the shots of the gun, they were sure that Steve had been killed or wounded. Monica began crying and the other three were all close to tears as the soldiers quickly pushed them along to their rooms. Somehow they had to try to contact Eclipse again. He was the only one that could help them now. They looked at each other and inconspicuously pointed to the communicators in their pockets.

One by one, each was rudely pushed into their rooms. More soldiers came and one went into each room. The entire barracks was surrounded with men, armed with automatic weapons. Tykesha wanted to go over and punch the soldier who had come in with her but she quickly came to her senses when a better idea came. She began taking off her blouse.

"Uh.. humm...." Tykesha said loudly to the guard who finally looked toward her. "I'm a little exhausted here. I'm trying to get undressed so I can go to bed and get some sleep. Do you mind, please?" She indicated for the man to turn around. They usually had sent female soldiers in with her, but this time, someone had made a mistake. The man turned around, embarrassed at seeing her with her blouse partially unbuttoned. Tykesha quickly took the small green crystal out of her pocket and got into her pajamas. She jumped into her bed and buried herself under the covers. "It's okay, you can turn around now."

The soldier turned around. Tykesha turned away from him and took the crystal communicator and began to whisper directly into it, hoping that the strength of her whisper would be sufficient to activate the device. "Eclipse can you hear me? It's Tykesha. We're in big trouble here. Summer has been kidnapped and taken outside of Baghdad in Iraq. She is to be killed if one of us don't come to Iraq and the military won't let any of us go. Steve escaped the barracks at Bill Air Force Base where the military is holding us captive. They fired a rifle twice at him. I'm afraid they may have..."

Suddenly the covers were pulled off of her. Tykesha quickly put the communicator under her pillow and turned over, her eyes meeting those of an angry soldier. "Who are you talking to?" barked the soldier.

"To God," Tykesha quickly responded, not believing how great her response had been. She quickly added another comment. "Don't you pray to God every night? That's what we're supposed to do, you know." The soldier sheepishly covered her up again and returned to his post at her door.

"Yes!" Tykesha whispered softly to herself. Then she decided that she had better pray, especially for Steve and for Summer.

Tom and Cheryl Solstice watched their television intently at the strange events that were transpiring at the main gate of the Air Force base. General Lever arrived at the gate and the reporters, and Amir's representative ran rapidly toward him. Men with remote cameras followed close behind. Portable lights had been placed to light the darkening area.

"General Lever, General Lever!" yelled the news correspondent. "This man here is General Kasafuut's representative

122

who has come to take one of Summer Solstice's friends to Iraq with him. Is it true that you are holding the five youth here?"

Microphones were pushed into the face of the General, who appeared quite nervous on the television screen. "I am not sure where General Kasafuut gets his information but it is completely incorrect. We are not holding Summer's five friends here. I have no idea where they are."

Tom Solstice heard nothing else. Rage grew within him at the lie that the General had just told to the world. He realized that if they didn't send one of his daughter's friends that she would be killed. He stood up quickly and stomped over to his telephone. His wife jumped in surprise.

"Where's the number to the CNV office in Salt Lake?" he asked his wife, rummaging through some drawers of the china cabinet. She leaped up to help him find the telephone book. Once she found it, she looked up the number and gave it to her husband. He lifted the receiver of his telephone and began to dial, unaware that a light was flashing in a government building in downtown Salt Lake City, alerting two government agents that the Solstice telephone was now being used. The agents were glued to the television set, unawares of the blinking light.

After three rings, a voice answered. "CNV, may I help you?"

"Yes, this is Mr. Solstice. General Lever is telling a lie...."

"Just one moment Mr. Solstice, I'll put you directly through to Mr. Duarte in New York."

The light continued flashing. The CNV correspondent asked General Lever many additional questions in an attempt to assess the truthfulness of the information given by General Kasafuut. He was successfully avoiding and denying the questions, indicating that he thought his story was a little far-fetched. The agents were engrossed in the proceedings. Tom Solstice was also viewing the proceedings as he waited for his telephone call to go through.

"This is Mr. Duarte. Can I help you Mr. Solstice?"

"Yes. General Lever lied about the youth being there. The story Kasafuut told is basically true."

The light continued flashing. One of the agents turned around to grab his cup of coffee and saw the light flashing. "Ron! Quick!

The Solstice telephone!" Sandwiches were dropped and earphones quickly acquired. "...Kasafuut told is basically true" were the only words that they heard. They turned white as sheets and quickly pushed a button, disconnecting Mr. Solstice's call to Mr. Duarte.

Mr. Solstice slammed down the telephone and cursed. His wife had never before heard him curse in his life. She waited for him to explain. Seeing her questioning glance he said, "Our line is being monitored. Someone disconnected me from my call."

She didn't believe him and lifted up the receiver to check the line. There was no dial tone. She clicked the button to the receiver several times. It was completely dead. "Maybe a telephone line is down?" she said.

Mr. Duarte was shocked with the news from Mr. Solstice. He contacted his secretary and asked her to look at her computer monitor for the telephone number of his most recent caller and return the call immediately. She pushed a computer button and the telephone number was automatically re-dialed. After a few moments a recording was activated. "The number you have reached is not in service at this time. Please check the number you are calling and try again." She manually dialed the number on the monitor with the same results.

The intercom buzzed. "Mr. Duarte, I get a recording indicating that the number is not in service."

"Thank you, Sandy. Please contact Bob at the Salt Lake office." Once the Salt Lake office was contacted, Mr. Duarte informed Bob of the new developments. "I think that Solstice's line is being monitored. During our call it was disconnected and is not in service now. You'd better get a crew over to the Solstice house right away."

"Already done it, Chief," Bob responded in a matter of fact way, obviously trying to impress his boss. "When the transmission from Kasafuut first came I assigned a crew to go and interview the parents. They should have already arrived by now." He was quite proud of his own work.

Steve managed to get to the pond area just as the men were coming over the hill. He found the water to be deep enough to immerse his whole body in the horizontal position. He took a deep breath and submerged himself.

"Where did he go?" the soldiers yelled as they ran up to the stream. They stopped and looked all around, their guns ready.

"He probably was just wounded and is trying to get to the main gate with all those television people there," the Colonel said authoritatively. Without waiting for a response from his two men he took out his hand-held two-way radio.

Steve could hold his breath no longer. He quietly raised his head above the water so that his mouth and nose were free to obtain a bit of fresh air. He heard the Colonel call for increased vigilance at the main gate to watch for the wounded young teenager. The Colonel looked around several times. Convinced that Steve was no longer in the area, he said, "Go back to the barracks. If the boy returns there I want him taken to the stockade area and I will personally deal with the brat." The men rapidly walked away, disappearing over the hill while the Colonel ran towards the gate.

Steve watched the direction that he headed. Once there was no one around, he painfully crawled over to the edge of the pond and climbed onto the dry shore that was still under the grove of pine trees. He remained motionless for a moment, considering his situation. He could no longer go to the main gate or to the barracks. His only hope was somehow to escape from the base itself. Then he remembered his communicator. He took it out of his pocket.

"I sure hope this works wet," he softly whispered to himself. "Eclipse, this is Steve. I've been shot and my only hope is to escape from this Air Force base. If you're close enough, we could sure use your help now."

He listened for any reply, but none came. In the stillness around him he remembered one of the things Eclipse had told them before they separated.

"Once I have completed my mission, I can create the computer program that will allow me to return to within two to four months of my leaving you on the ridge."

"Months", was repeated over and over in his head. He began to cry. He was sure that Eclipse had not even had time to complete his mission, let alone create the computer program to return to the appropriate time period on earth.

125

CHAPTER 9

The sound of doors slamming shut in front of the Solstice home caused Tom Solstice to walk to his front room and peek carefully out of the window in his front door.

"CNV is here!" he called loudly to his wife.

He opened the front door. As he did, he saw a line of military personnel standing in front of his front gate, in between his home and the CNV news team. The soldiers were armed with automatic weapons that were pointed at the news team. He couldn't believe what he saw. He ran toward his gate and opened it. Suddenly, one of the soldiers turned and pointed his weapon at Mr. Solstice and walked toward him.

"Go ahead! Kill me! In front of the entire world!"

The soldier stopped. Tom Solstice noticed that the news team had brought their cameras and portable lights out. They were pointed toward him and the soldier. "What are you doing here." He looked up and down the line of soldiers. "Get off of my property!" he yelled, cursing at the soldiers.

An officer appeared from nowhere and put his hand on the weapon of the soldier and pushed it out of Mr. Solstice's face. "Mr. Solstice, let's be reasonable. We are assigned to protect you and your wife. Please let us do our job."

"Protect?" Mr. Solstice's voice was loud and he was out of breath from the tenseness of the situation. "Do you call bugging my telephone and disconnecting my call to CNV protecting me? Is CNV going to hurt us? Search them! Where are their weapons?"

"Mr. Solstice, this is not..."

Tom Solstice interrupted the officer. "Let me tell you what you're doing. General Lever has just lied to the world about the location of Summer's friends. They are at the base. And why did he lie?" Distance microphones were trained on the conversation. The broadcast was beamed live throughout the entire world. "Because you want to keep them for yourself to learn the secrets of super light travel. Meanwhile my Summer will be sacrificed by Amir! Get your soldiers out of here now! I'm walking through these men and will talk to the CNV team! They seem to be more interested in the truth than you!"

He started walking. Twenty rifles were turned on him, ready to fire. Cheryl Solstice watched in horror as her husband walked closer to the line of men. He stared coolly at the ones nearest him. Closer and closer he came. He could see fear in the eyes of the men closest to him. His eyes burned with anger and determination. He made contact with their rifles and grabbed them, pushing them into the air. Without hesitation, he walked through the line of men toward the CNV trucks. His wife breathed a sigh of relief. Her legs became weak, forcing her to sit on the front porch while she watched what was occurring. The audio from her television set could clearly be heard through the open front door.

Amir sat watching the CNV news channel. Summer was in her room, also watching on a television that was provided for her. With the confirmation of the location of Summer's friends at the base by Mr. Solstice, the Baghdad CNV correspondent was notified that his team was to stay on site, ready to get General Kasafuut's response to what was happening. Summer was proud of her father's courage and longed to be beside him as he seemed to fight against an unbeatable enemy. She just didn't know if the enemy was Iraq or the United States military. Maybe it was both.

Her father was now explaining about the journey of the six teenagers through the universe and about Summer's abduction by Iraq. Amir appeared to be nervous at this point of the broadcast. After Tom Solstice's explanation and answering questions from the CNV reporter, the reporter turned toward the camera and said, "We now go to Baghdad to get General Amir Kasafuut's responses to Mr. Solstice's comments."

The CNV Baghdad correspondent warned the General not to use the air time to make any other threats toward anyone's life or he would never again get the opportunity to speak internationally, no matter what the reason. The General nodded agreement. Transmission was begun.

"We are live outside of Baghdad, Iraq. General Kasafuut, would you tell us your impression of what General Lever said about not knowing the location of Summer's friends."

"It is obvious, from Mr. Solstice, that I told the truth. Why the General lied about Summer's friends is also clear to me. Any country would love to have the knowledge of the space ship's power source. It could solve the energy shortage of the entire world. The United States would like to have it as much as we or any other country in the world."

"If only you had the power, then you could control the world, isn't that correct?" The correspondent looked Amir in the eyes.

Amir did not seem affected by the question. "That is an easy question to answer. It is yes. That is why the United States is holding the five teenagers prisoner on Bill Air Force Base."

"Is that why you kidnapped Summer Solstice, General? Two government agents were wounded in the kidnapping. Did you know that?"

This time, Amir moved nervously in his chair. He knew he could not confess to kidnapping a United States citizen. He thought quickly before he responded. "I was completely unaware of the way in which Summer got here. I was notified that she would be visiting my country. It has been a privilege to have this young lady here."

The correspondent did not believe Amir's last comment. He was about to ask another question when a message was received from CNV on his earphone. "Thank you General. We will return to Bill Air Force Base to talk to General Lever."

The sky was now getting dark. The coolness of the evening air caused chills to pass through Steve's body. The flesh wound was painful and had clotted onto his pants so that any movement of his leg would pull on his skin and wound, increasing the pain. The sky suddenly became illuminated with bright lights in the direction of the main gate. Steve assumed that it was from the CNV news team. Somehow he had to get to them... and it had to be now. He looked at the stream. It came from about two hundred yards to the south of the lights in the sky. He wondered if there would be any chance that he could follow the stream to where it left the base and escape.

"No use wondering. It's now or never," he whispered softly to himself, trying to get the courage to begin moving toward the perimeter fence of the base. Steve tried to stand up but found it too painful for his left leg to hold up his weight, especially from the tugging of his pants on his skin. He looked down and saw that his wound was now connected to his pants with clotted blood as glue. He quickly got back down on his knees and began to crawl along the side of the stream like a toddler. He stopped once in a while to listen for anyone approaching his location. It wasn't long before the base's perimeter fence was in full view. He could barely see the stream disappear underneath the fence. He prayed that there would be room enough for him to submerge his body and to pull it underneath the fence. He could see, from where he was crawling, that occasionally, there were areas where the stream became fairly deep... at least two feet in some places. He looked up and down the fence to see if there were any soldiers or dogs patrolling the perimeter. No movement could be seen.

Taking a deep breath, he started crawling the remaining fifty yards to the fence. To his left about two hundred yards, the CNV news cameras and lights could be clearly seen at the main gate. To his right, about half a mile, the whining of the tires of the traffic on the freeway that led to Salt Lake City pierced the early evening air. Only thirty yards left to the fence!

"Can anyone get under the fence through the stream, Captain?" The unique, gruff voice of the Colonel came from behind him. Steve froze, his heart beating wildly. He looked around. He could barely make out the outline of two men walking toward him. They walked without flashlights. He began to panic. There were no trees near him, so his only hope to escape detection was the stream, but now there was not enough daylight in the sky to see how deep the stream was. He would surely be seen!

"No sir. The electricity in the fence will kill anyone who touches it. The stream is not even a foot deep at that point. Steve is too big of a boy to clear that small distance."

They were only thirty yards from tripping over Steve. He decided to chance rolling into the middle of the stream. Taking a deep breath, he rolled over, slowly, twice, returning to the icy water. He lay still, face down in the stream, but found that the water covered all but two or three inches of the top part of his body. His hands and face began to feel numb. It was too late to make another movement. They walked up to within five yards of where Steve lay.

130

His body seemed to take the shape of a protruding rock.

The Colonel was beginning to look strangely at the form in the middle of the stream, when a call came on his two-way radio. "Colonel, the General needs you at the gate immediately. It's beginning to get wild out here. Solstice confirmed Amir's accusation about the lies he told. General Lever tried to implicate the President for his decision to lie but President Ohm has denied ever talking to him." The two men quickly turned toward the main gate and ran.

Steve lifted his head out of the water and looked around him. The two officers were almost at the main gate. He breathed in great gulps of air. "Great! The fence is electrified!" Steve said to himself. He decided to chance it anyway. As he pushed himself up in order to crawl to the side of the stream, his hand went deeply into silt…at least two feet. Maybe there would be some silt at the fence that he could dig away to safely get under the fence. He realized that he would need a depth of at least two feet to get under the fence and even that would be extremely risky. Maybe he could get it even deeper if there was enough silt.

Within three minutes, after arriving at the perimeter fence, Steve found himself in the stream once again. He hopefully pushed his hand into the bottom of the stream. His heart sank. The silt wasn't as deep as at the spot where he was trying to hide from the Colonel…only about a foot. He began to dig with his hands, removing rocks and silt as fast as he could. Every once in a while he could hear people yelling at the main gate. He wondered if he could get out in time to get to the news team. With each handful removed, it seemed that the stream would bring in more material. He couldn't give up now. It was his only hope to save his life and the life of his friends.

Steve felt under the fence. He estimated with his arm that it was a little over a foot and a half under the surface of the stream. With renewed effort, he continued removing small pebbles and dirt. Finally, he reached solid material and could dig no further. He made another estimate…not quite two feet. He looked at the fence. The bottom of the fence was about an inch above the surface of the stream. He breathed heavily from the effort made to dig in the ice-

131

cold water. He cupped his hands and blew on them to try to warm them up. He was not successful and started to shiver. He put his hands back into the water and felt the bottom of the stream, hoping to find something else to remove. He groaned from pain and discouragement. Finally, he decided to make the attempt, no matter what the outcome. He and his friends had to be saved at all costs.

He laid down on his back in the large depression that he had cleared, with his head toward the fence. He took a deep breath as his head went below the water. He felt the front part of his shirt float to the surface of the stream. He took his hand and pushed it down. His hand was slightly above the surface of the water. Was it enough to clear the fence? He began to push with his legs but the pain in his left leg prevented him from pushing with enough force to cause him to move under the fence. He realized that he would need both hands as well. He lifted his head to replenish his lungs with oxygen and took a deep breath and submerged it once again. He removed his hand from his shirt and it floated to the top of the water. He pushed with all of his might and moved slightly. His face was under the fence, his nose barely clearing the electrified metal. Another heroic shove and his neck passed under the fence. On the third shove he only moved half of the distance between his neck and waist. He pushed again, this time becoming conscious of his shirt preventing him from moving. The horror of the situation dawned on him. His shirt was caught on the bottom of the fence. He knew he could last only a short time more under the water, but realized that when he came up for air this time, he would come into contact with the fence. Steve's mind raced wildly, not knowing what to do next. He quickly decided that he had to reach up and pull his shirt down. He did so, half expecting for his hand to touch the fence. When it didn't he gained hope. He grabbed his shirt and pulled it down. Then he lifted the torso of his body up slightly and tucked as much of the shirt under his back as he could. This time, the shirt did not float up. But now, Steve's lungs were crying for air. With all of the strength that he could muster, he pushed again. His waist was now under the fence. He pushed again, moving himself another four inches. He couldn't stand it any longer. He knew that he had to surface to get air. He carefully began lifting his head out of the water. As his nose and mouth cleared he drank in huge amounts of air. He breathed in and out heavily for at least a minute. He could see that if he sat up straight, that his waist would touch the fence. He went under the water once again and pushed again. He moved slightly. After two more pushes, all but his feet had cleared the fence. He sat completely up and then carefully pulled his feet toward him. The shoelace of his left shoe became entangled on the bottom of the fence. He tried to move his foot back and then pull it out again, but found it to be hopelessly trapped.

"I have to get the shoe off somehow," he said out loud to himself. He tried to put his right foot under his left heel but found it pushing his left foot up. It would soon touch the fence. He changed positions so that his right foot was at the side and a little bit under his heel. He pushed and began to feel it move, but the pain of his wound increased dramatically. He almost screamed out loud, but put his arm in his mouth and bit with all of his might. One last push and his shoe finally came off. It fell into the water and began to float. It bumped against the fence...nothing happened. The current caused it to change position slightly. Steve had now pulled himself out of the water. He watched the shoe move back and forth and bump the fence repeatedly. Wasn't there any electricity at all? At that moment, the metallic eyelet of the shoe touched the fence, sending sparks flying in all directions. A siren began to sound on the base.

Steve jumped with fear. He turned on his knees and continued to crawl as fast as he could toward the main gate. Lights went on around the perimeter of the base where Steve had made his escape. He was in full view now. He continued crawling. Hearing sirens of military police he decided to endure the pain. He stood rapidly and the clot, now loosened by the wetness of his pants, separated from the skin, tearing the scab completely off of the wound, exposing the sensitive skin. He screamed out loud in pain, tears coming to his eyes. He began to run with a limp, his left foot now bare, was exposed to the rocks and occasional pieces of broken glass that cut the bottom of his feet.

"There he is!" came a cry from the other side of the fence. "He's running toward the main gate." They called to the gate and a small army headed there.

Steve was now only seventy-five yards from the main gate. Some of the CNV news team had turned around to look at the commotion that was occurring behind them. They saw a young man running toward them with a limp. Some of the portable lights were turned toward the young man. When Steve saw the lights on him he began to yell at the top of his lungs. "Help me! They tried to kill me!" He continued running. Forty- five yards...thirty- five. Seven military police jeeps came out of the front gate and turned toward Steve.

"My name is Steve!" he yelled. "I'm one of Summer's friends!"

The number of reporters from different television stations and newspapers from the cities around the base had increased to over thirty. When they heard who he was, they began to sprint toward Steve. Cameras turned away from the General and began to follow the army of military police and reporters. The jeeps had caught up to the reporters and were just passing them when they converged on the young man. Steve collapsed on the ground from exhaustion. His bloody pant leg was clearly seen by the reporters. The military police, with the Colonel at their lead had stopped the jeep and surrounded Steve. They grabbed him and pulled him off the ground and tried to get him to stand on his own. By then, reporters and television cameras surrounded them. The Colonel and his men began to drag him toward one of the jeeps. The reporters crowded around them, which made it almost impossible to move.

"Please don't let them take me!" Steve cried out suddenly. "I'm one of Summer's friends. We are all being held under guard on the base!" A cry of outrage came from the press. They took advantage of their number and completely halted the progress of the military police.

A CNV reporter cried out into his microphone, while a television camera broadcast the event worldwide. "Steve has been wounded. How did it happen kid?"

With the cameras trained on the Colonel's men, and Steve's latest cry for help, the military police became less and less energetic in their attempts to drag him away. When the reporter asked the question, they froze. The Colonel glared at Steve threateningly.

Steve ignored his silent threat. "The Colonel here," he said indicating to the man beside him, "ordered that his men shoot me when I tried to escape from the barracks where we're all held prisoners. I overheard him tell his men that if I was caught to take me to the stockade and that he would deal with me personally."

Steve's body suddenly went limp and he collapsed on the ground. The Colonel immediately responded. "Clear a path quickly, so we can get him to the base infirmary."

The reporters refused to move. One of the reporters with his cellular telephone still in his hand said, "I've already called emergency and they'll be here in five minutes. If you take him in the base how do we know that you won't harm him more?"

"Clear these reporters," the Colonel commanded to his men. The military police took out their clubs and began to push the reporters but the reporters pushed back and refused to move. The military police removed their guns from their holsters.

The CNV reporter pushed through some of the Colonel's men and shoved his microphone near the mouth of the Colonel. "Are you going to shoot us, too, Colonel? The entire world wants to know your answer?"

The Colonel tensed and made a decision to use force. He removed his gun and pointed it at the reporter. Amir's representative watched at a distance in disbelief. Just then, General Lever pushed through the crowd and came up to the Colonel.

"Stop Colonel, the President of the United States has ordered this whole thing to stop now. Let Steve be taken to the local hospital for treatment." Sirens could be heard in the distance. A police car and ambulance rounded the bend and came to a screeching halt at the outskirts of the crowd. Two other cars were coming to the gate and stopped close to the ambulance. Several men and women emerged from the cars. They were the families of Steve, Jose, Monica, Tykesha and Maria. Cheryl Solstice had gone to the neighbors to use their telephone to notify the families of her daughter's friends to go to the gate of the base to attempt to put pressure on the General to release their children. They had continued following the reports on a portable television brought in each of the cars. The unexpected turn of events, with the appearance

135

of Steve, had caused them to break all speed limits to get to the base quickly. Steve's father ran and pushed through the crowd. He came up to his son who was being placed on a stretcher to be taken to the hospital. Bottles of chemicals hung by him and dripped into his veins as paramedics lifted the stretcher and carried it to the ambulance. Steve's dad followed and got into the ambulance with his son. It sped away, its lights flashing and siren sounding loudly. The Colonel and his men and the reporters watched as the ambulance disappeared around a curve in the road.

Summer was horrified at the treatment Steve had received. She wanted more than ever to be with her parents and friends. Amir laughed inwardly at the embarrassment to the US military and government. He knew that when the President of the United States had denied talking to the General, that it too had been a lie and that it would be only a short time until the American people would demand justice for the way that the five teenagers were treated. Perhaps now his representative would be able to bring the youth with the communicator to Iraq. He rubbed his hands with satisfaction.

General Lever turned to the reporters. "I would like to make a statement." Silence fell on the entire group. "I would like to apologize for the way in which Colonel Lam behaved. He took upon himself authority that was not within his right. These young people were to be protected from suffering the same fate as that of Summer, not to be treated as prisoners. We felt that the best way to prevent foreign powers from taking them would be to keep them all in one group. I was unaware of the shooting of the boy and of the way the Colonel had treated and threatened to harm him if he was caught. He shall be disciplined severely according to military law." The General paused for a moment as if he had forgotten to say something. Deciding that he had said all that could be said at that time, he thanked the reporters and started to walk away.

"General, what about sending the youth and communicator to Iraq so that Summer will not be killed?"

The General stopped and turned toward the reporter, who held a microphone in readiness. "Son, I'm going to return the other four youth to their parents and will let them make the decision. The youth are packing their belongings and will be released to their parents care in fifteen minutes."

A jeep came out of the main gate. Four teenagers were already yelling and waving with their loved ones in view. The jeep stopped and the youth got out. Military personnel carried their belongings and placed them near the cars. Tears of happiness and hugs were captured for the world to see. Then everyone became silent as the four youth huddled in a little circle. Jose began to speak but Tykesha interrupted him before he could begin. "I'm going to go to Iraq and take the communicator to Summer."

"That's not what we decided," Jose glared.

Tykesha ignored him. Secretly, he really didn't want to go and so did not put up much resistance. Tykesha walked over to her parents. "Mom and Dad. May I go and help out Summer?"

Her parents looked at each other, worry written in their expressions. They couldn't bear the thought of letting their daughter go to Iraq, but they also couldn't bear the thought of Summer being killed because Tykesha did not go to her. They nodded their approval and then they embraced together for a long moment. They stepped back and Tykesha picked up her bags. Amir's representative took the bags from her hand and escorted her to his limousine. The driver placed the bags in the back and opened the doors for the two riders. Soon, the limousine started and carefully turned around and drove toward the Salt Lake International Airport.

CHAPTER 10

"Summer!" Tykesha cried as she saw her friend, after the blindfold was removed from her eyes. They ran and gave each other a hug, tears of joy in their eyes. The overpowering feelings of fear and foreboding gripped their hearts.

Amir stood watching the happy reunion. Soon he became bored and walked up to the two girls. "It is time to begin," he said coolly. "Tykesha, please give me your communicator."

Tykesha hesitated and looked at Summer. "It's okay, Tykesha." Tykesha removed the small green crystalline communicator from her pocket and gave it to the General.

Amir looked confused. He turned the crystal over and over in his hand and then held it close to his eye and tried to look through it with a light behind it. Then he looked at Summer and frowned. "What is this, Summer? You described to me a small metallic object, not a green crystal."

"I didn't tell you the truth about the communicator at first, General. I wasn't sure what I could tell you at first, especially since you had just kidnapped me."

Amir hesitated for a few seconds while he studied Summer's face. Then he spoke. "How does it work?"

"You hold it close to your mouth and speak into it. Call the name of our friend, Maria, and then identify yourself and tell her you wish to talk to her. She should be at home right now. She must just be getting out of bed at about this time"

"I thought that you said that there was only one communicator with your friends?"

"Another lie. Maria has one, too."

"Did you lose your communicator, or is that a lie, too."

"I lost it when I was kidnapped, General."

Satisfied, Amir held the communicator close to his mouth. "Maria, this is General Amir Kasafuut." Amir waited for ten seconds but nothing happened. He looked in a questioning manner at Summer.

"Try again, General. Maria should be fairly close to her

communicator, unless the soldiers at Bill Air Force Base got it." She looked at Tykesha.

"Those idiots didn't get any... I mean, didn't get Maria's communicator." Tykesha had just about said that they didn't get any of their communicators, but quickly changed her story. It dawned on her that Summer must still have her own communicator. *Summer's afraid to give up her only link to the outside world and to Eclipse,* she thought to herself.

Before the General could say anything, Maria's voice was clearly heard. "This is Maria, General Kasafuut. Did Tykesha get there okay?"

The General, shocked at the clarity and strength of the signal, responded. "Yes Maria. Both she and Summer are just fine."

"How can I believe you if I can't hear their voices?"

"Your friend Maria is as skeptical as you are, Summer." He handed the communicator to her.

"I'm okay, Maria... and so is Tykesha." The General reached for the communicator and Summer handed it to him.

"Summer was just showing me how this works. I must admit that I doubted that such a small instrument could work. I must stop the transmission, Maria."

"How do I turn it off?" the General asked Summer.

"Just stop speaking into it."

"Now is the real test. To call your friend Eclipse, I follow the same procedure, correct?"

"Yes, but don't expect Eclipse to answer you. Many times on the planet we went to, I called Eclipse and he was so busy he didn't have time to answer me."

"Sit down girls." The sinister tone in Amir's voice caused the girls to tremble with trepidation about his plans.

"General, if you're going to call Eclipse and ask him to come to Iraq you need to know that it could take between two to four months for him to respond," Tykesha explained.

"Be quiet...both of you!" The girls looked away momentarily from the ugly expression on his face. "I'm not sure that you are telling me the truth." He brought the communicator to his mouth and began to speak. "Eclipse, this is General Amir Kasafuut,

Minister of Defense of Iraq. I have Summer and Tykesha as prisoners and will give them to you in exchange for the secret of the power source of your space ship so that we can duplicate it here on earth. You must arrive within one week or I will kill both of them. If you have not arrived by five o'clock in the afternoon seven days from now, they shall both die." He waited for at least two or three minutes and no response came.

Amir put the communicator into his pocket and went to his desk and buzzed his secretary. In his native tongue, he asked the secretary to get the two girls and lock them in Summer's room. He instructed him that they were not to leave the room at any time, not even to eat. Food would have to be taken to them by the cafeteria staff.

Summer and Tykesha were horrified. They were almost positive that Eclipse could not arrive in such a short time. The secretary came in and motioned for the girls to follow him. Before they left the General's office, Tykesha turned and asked the General if she could have her communicator back. He laughed diabolically and yelled at the girls to get out of the office.

The secretary led Summer and Tykesha to her room. Summer breathed a sigh of relief that they would not be separated. Once inside the room, the secretary closed the door and locked it from the outside with a large padlock. When they heard the lock shut them in, Summer and Tykesha sprang to the door and grabbed the doorknob. It turned easily, but as they tried to open the door, it wouldn't budge. They were trapped!

"At least they don't have soldiers standing inside and outside the room," Tykesha commented in a discouraged manner.

"Is that what they did to you when you were at the base, Tykesha?" Tykesha looked at her friend and nodded her head. Summer shuddered at the thought of her friends being treated like prisoners in their own country.

Summer sat down on the chair by her bed and Tykesha sat on the only bed in the room. She looked at the small couch on the other side of the room. "I guess that's where I'll be sleeping," Tykesha commented. There was no response for the two girls just sat and stared into space, wondering what would happen to them in seven days if Eclipse was unable to return.

"Do you suppose this room is bugged?" Summer stood up and began looking around the room.

Tykesha got up and followed her. They said nothing more to each other as they began to look underneath and behind all of the furniture and in all areas of the bathroom. Finding nothing, Summer indicated silently for Tykesha to stand close to her. Tykesha didn't understand why Summer wanted her to do it, but she went along with the request. When Tykesha was within a foot of her friend, she saw Summer slowly reach into her pocket and pull her communicator out. Tykesha smiled when she saw it. Summer closed her hand around the communicator and walked away from Tykesha and sat down on the bed. Then, using the hand containing the communicator to prop up her chin, she "pretended" to talk to Eclipse.

"Eclipse, oh how I wish you were here with Tykesha and me and would <u>come within a week</u>. If only I had my communicator to call you and to listen to your voice so it would take away the boredom of being <u>locked in my room</u>." Summer kept her hand on her chin and said nothing for a few minutes. Then she stood up and walked toward Tykesha. As she walked, she put her hands into both of her pockets. When she reached Tykesha, she released the communicator and pulled her hands slowly out of her pockets and then stretched.

"Boy, I'm sleepy," Summer said as she forced a yawn. "I think I'm going to take a nap for awhile." She went over to her bed and laid down and closed her eyes.

The nurse wheeled Steve out of the hospital on the afternoon of the next day. His parents followed him. The nurse brought Steve close to the back door of his car and opened it. She helped him move the short distance from the wheelchair to the car. He groaned from the pain that remained from his wound, the cuts in his left foot and from the soreness of his muscles. The nurse smiled and then closed the door and waved at Steve. His mother and father got into the front. After starting the car, they began driving down the long, thin, deserted country road that led to the freeway. The road passed through several thick groves of aspen trees and small pines.

As they neared one of the groves of trees, Steve noticed a car traveling extremely close behind them. "Dad, there's a car behind us that seems to be in a hurry. Maybe we'd better pull over and let it by?"

His father looked in the rear view mirror and began to slow and pull over to the side of the road. He came to a full stop. It seemed strange that the car did not pass them. He looked around and saw that it had stopped behind them and that four men had gotten out and were walking toward their car. Steve looked back at the same time and felt uneasy. He turned around and, as he looked to the front of his parent's car, saw another car rapidly approaching them from the opposite direction. It stopped in front of them and two men with automatic weapons got out of the car.

"Oh no!" Steve yelled. At the same time his father pushed down the accelerator and began to pull his car around the one in front of him. The two men opened fire. Small explosions could be heard from the tires in front of the car and the back and it rocked and bumped as it continued at a much slower pace. His father did not stop the car but kept on driving to try to escape from impending doom. Rat…a…tat…tat. Several rounds were pumped directly toward the front of the car. The car shuddered as the high-powered bullets entered the electric motor and the hood popped open, making it impossible for Steve's dad to see where he was driving. The car finally came to a stop.

Two of the men behind the car rushed up and pulled open the back door nearest Steve while the other two ran and pointed their weapons at Steve's parents. The two men who had arrived in the other car stood behind those guarding the frightened parents. All six had nylon stockings pulled over their heads. "Do not move and we will not hurt you," the man pointing a revolver at the head of Steve's father said, in a thick accent. Then he barked commands to the two men who, by now, were forcing Steve out of the car. He spoke in a foreign language that none of the family recognized. He felt helpless as he was dragged toward the car behind him. The two men shoved Steve into the center of the back seat and sat on either side of him, closing and locking the doors. The two men holding guns on Steve's parents returned to the car, removed their nylon stockings and quickly drove away toward the freeway. The two men

143

that had stopped the car with their weapons remained still as the other car drove away. They pointed their guns threateningly at Steve's parents who did not dare to move an inch. After five minutes the men suddenly turned and ran to their car. It whirled around, its rear wheels digging into the dirt at the side of the road, sped off and disappeared into the grove of trees in front of them.

Shaken and frightened, Steve's father took out their cellular telephone and dialed emergency. When the operator answered, he described their situation and the police were dispatched immediately. He then dialed Maria's house to warn her mother about the potential danger her daughter might be in. He asked her to call Jose's home when he heard the "low-battery" beeper sound on his telephone and the transmission was automatically terminated.

"Goodbye Mom, I'll be back after Monica and I go shopping at the mall," Maria yelled to her mother as she opened the front door.

"Be back before dark, Maria," her mother called from the washroom.

"Okay, Mom!" She was so grateful that she was no longer followed by the blood hounds of the government that she didn't notice the features of a man who was strolling slowly by the front of her house as she came out. Except for the great aging that had occurred with her mother and the plight of Tykesha and Summer, she almost felt like everything was back to normal in her life. She ran out of the door and walked quickly down the sidewalks and through the alleys that led to Monica's home, less than half a mile away.

Within five minutes, she was standing on Monica's porch, ringing her doorbell. Monica opened the door and let her in. "I'll be ready in a minute. Just have to comb my hair." Monica disappeared into her bathroom and Maria followed her. Neither spoke, although they both were worried about the same things. Would they ever get back to their own time? Would they ever see Tykesha and Summer alive again? Would they have to worry about the safety of their lives for the rest of the time that they would live on this planet? Each tried to hide their fears from the other and hoped that a trip to the mall would help them forget about the worries that they had.

Monica left the bathroom and ran to her mother's bedroom

where she was cleaning. "Maria and I are going to the mall, Mom. We'll be back before dark."

Her mother looked concerned. "The last time you said that you were going somewhere with your friends, Doug Volcano took you to the mountains and you were taken to another planet. Are you sure it's the mall you're going to?"

Monica giggled. "Yes, Mom. It's really the mall, this time." Her mother gave her a hug and kiss and watched her daughter walk out of the front door with Maria.

Monica was telling Maria of her mother's comment as they turned down the sidewalk and headed to the mall, three-quarters of a mile away. As they neared a big, empty field that stood in between them and the mall, Monica said, "Hey, Maria, if we cut across the field, we'll cut off half the distance. What do you say?"

"I'm always ready to save a little work in walking," Maria laughed as they turned into the field. It was covered with tall grass that had grown from the large amount of rain that had occurred during the two weeks prior to their returning to earth. They breathed in the fresh late afternoon air as they walked quickly in a direct line to the mall. They could see it clearly and were not more than two-tenths of a mile from dress and shoe shops, food stores and boys. A helicopter hovered silently overhead.

Monica looked around to see how far they had walked. She was shocked to see two men following them. "Maria, I think we're being followed," she said with alarm.

Maria turned around to see the two men behind them begin to run toward them. "Let's get out of here, Monica!" she yelled, sprinting toward the mall. Monica responded immediately and was not more than a step or two behind her. They were only two hundred and fifty yards from reaching the pavement of the parking lot to the mall. The distance was closing quickly, but so were the men. They ran as fast as they could, glancing behind them occasionally to see the men still closing the distance between them.

"Run faster, Maria, run faster!" Monica yelled, becoming weary from her tremendous effort.

"I'm trying," Maria responded. "We've got to make it!" The men were only twenty yards behind them. The distance to the parking lot was less than seventy-five yards. As the girls continued running, the helicopter that was overhead suddenly lowered and landed on the ground just in front of the parking lot. The girls thought that it was strange for a helicopter to be there, but kept on running. Suddenly, two men jumped from the helicopter and started running toward them. Maria and Monica turned to the right, parallel to the mall, and continued running. It was no use. The men from the helicopter were only two yards from grabbing them. Maria tripped and fell to the ground and Monica stopped to help her get up. They felt strong hands grab their arms and were about to scream, when the hard, cold point of a deadly weapon was shoved into each of their sides.

"Quiet or the two of you shall die now!" a man gruffly said from behind them, with a strong accent. The girls were pulled towards the helicopter and as they reached it, saw a group of people in the parking lot staring at them.

The hands of the men holding the girls gripped their arms with much more force, causing them to cry out in pain. "Do not say anything, or this will be the last that you see your parents for the rest of your lives." The girls stopped struggling. No one from the crowd tried to come to their assistance. They just stared.

Once the girls were in the helicopter with the two men, it took off and headed towards the mountains to the west of the valley. In the distance, they could see a police car with its lights flashing as it headed toward the mall. After, Steve's father had called Maria's mother and told her that his son had been kidnapped, she immediately called the police, explaining the danger to her daughter and Monica.

The telephone rang in Jose's home and his mother went to answer it in the back of the house. It was Maria's mother. At exactly the same time the front doorbell rang. Jose went to answer the door. He looked outside the front window as he neared the door and saw a US mail truck. He saw a man with a uniform on. It looked like the mailman. He opened it and the man politely introduced himself as having a special delivery package.

"Jose! Come and get away from the door immediately!" His mother appeared in the front room. He had never seen her run so fast as long as he could remember. It impressed him so much that he turned around and walked toward her, without thinking about what she had said.

"What did you say, Mom?"

"Jose, did you invite that man into the house?"

Jose whirled around. The mailman had entered their home without being invited, certainly strange behavior for someone who was supposed to be delivering a package.

"Please leave our home now," Jose demanded but the man didn't move. Instead he produced a revolver with a silencer on it.

"I said for you to come away from the door, Jose. Maria's mother told me that Steve has been kidnapped."

The man moved closer. "I believe that it would be in your best interest to come with me, Jose," the man said with an accent.

"And if I refuse?"

"Then I will kill you now. It makes no difference to me if I deliver you dead or alive. I still get my money." Jose's mother started weeping and screaming.

"Stand there or you and your mother are dead!" He walked over to the woman and took out a scarf and gagged her so she could not yell or scream. He then tied her hands behind her back and fastened her to a metal light pole attached from their ceiling to their floor. She continued to struggle and, after a moment, became still as she passed out from stress.

"I suggest that you walk outside and get into the back of the truck. He put his gun underneath his uniform and came up beside Jose who was a full foot smaller. The man grabbed Jose's arm with his other hand and escorted him to the truck. The back door opened and Jose got in. An accomplice, dressed in a suit, was waiting for him in the back of the truck. Jose was tied and gagged and thrown to the floor of the truck as it traveled quickly down the street.

The mail truck approached a deserted stretch of smooth salt flats, about ten miles from the Great Salt Lake. As they hurried along, the driver and his companion saw the forms of a helicopter, jet and a car get bigger and bigger. When they arrived, they could see their comrades pacing back and forth with nervousness. When the truck stopped they ran and opened the back and carried Jose to

147

the jet. They watched as Jose was carried to a seat near the rear of the airplane. Once secure, the occupants of the airplane waved and closed the door to the jet as it began to prepare to take off. Within seconds the engines began to whine as they received greater power. The brakes of the jet were released and it increased in speed until it lifted off of the ground. Once airborne, it headed south. After disappearing into the horizon, the delivery truck, car and helicopter quickly left in different directions.

Jose was afraid to speak as he felt the jet take off. He was sure they had been kidnapped by some foreign power, greedy for the secret energy source of the transporter. As he looked around the cabin of the jet, what he saw caused him to shake in fear. On the seats beside and in front of him, Maria, Monica, and Steve were gagged and tied, each in a separate seat. Seat belts held each of them securely during takeoff. They had all been kidnapped at almost the same time. They looked at each other, communicating the same message. Where were they going? What country wanted the secret of Eclipse's power source? Were they going to get out of this alive? They knew they didn't have the answers to the questions and were glad that they didn't. They just had to wait and see what would happen.

Jose could see the heads of several men and one woman closer to the front of the cabin in the jet. Who were they? He did not have long to wait. One of the men got up and walked toward the back where the teenagers sat. The man saw the frightened look on the faces of the youth. After a few moments he spoke to them. "I want you to know," he said with an accent that made it hard for the youth to understand him, "that if you cooperate with us that you will not be harmed but will be returned to your families. Those who do not cooperate with us will be killed." He untied their hands and took the gags out of their mouths. Then, turning around, he walked back to his seat at the front of the jet. After several hours of flying, some of the adults at the front of the cabin unbuckled their seat belts and stood up for a break.

The four teenagers sat quietly, listening to the sound of the whine of the two jet engines, not daring to say a word. They watched the movements of their kidnappers. Occasionally they

148

would look back at them, but each time they did, the teenagers turned their eyes to the floor. Suddenly, the entire jet shook. A loud sound like a spark of electricity cracked through their ears. So great was the unexpected movement of the airplane that the men and women at the front of the cabin were thrown to the floor. Some were knocked unconscious. Those who weren't, attempted to crawl towards their seats. As the jet took another sudden downward turn, they fell back to the front of the airplane and remained there, unable to stand or pull themselves to their seats.

The hearts of the four teenagers were pounding. Jose was closest to the window and looked out. A huge arc of electricity connected the left engine with another part of the body of the jet. Suddenly the arc disappeared and the airplane banked left as it continued down.

"I think we're going to crash," Jose said, almost unable to breathe. The others froze in terror. They wondered when they would hit the ground. The rapid decrease in altitude was causing their ears to pop and the youth continually yawned to be able to hear. The airplane banked to the right.

"There's huge, snow-covered mountains down there, and they're coming up fast," Maria screamed in panic.

The whine of the engines became louder and louder and then suddenly became silent. The youth held their breath as they watched themselves approach the mountaintops. "Keep your seat belts on," Steve yelled. The pilot attempted to bring the airplane to a more level position. Seconds later the jet crashed into the side of a snow and ice covered mountain ridge. As the jet hit the ground, the grinding of the snow and ice on the bottom of the airplane seemed as loud as the earthquake on Magma. Had they not had their seat belts on, they would have been catapulted to the front of the cabin and crushed to death. As it was, they screamed in pain as their seat belts dug into their stomachs and waists. They prayed that their lives would be spared. The jet hit a huge boulder protruding from the snow and the right wing was torn off. The youth lost consciousness. The jet began to spin around and then it came to rest on the side of an icy, steep ridge. The adults, who were in the front of the cabin, lay still on the floor. The four teenagers also made no movement.

149

The howl of the wind was loud outside the airplane and the temperature inside began to decrease. The sun had disappeared in the western horizon and darkness began to cover the icy, snow-covered peaks and ridges.

The sun peeked over the eastern mountains as Maria awoke in the thirty-three degree cabin temperature. She had nothing to cover herself and her entire body felt icy cold. She tried to move and groaned with pain in her stomach and shoulders. She looked around at the others in the cabin. There was no movement.

"Steve!" She looked across the isle and he began to stir a little but did not wake up. "Steve," she said much louder. This time Steve's eyes opened and Monica and Jose began to stir.

"Oh…I ache all over," Steve groaned in pain. "Where are we?"

"On top of a mountain ridge." Maria eyed the steep angle of the airplane on the ridge and wondered what was keeping it from sliding off of the mountain.

"Monica, Maria, are you okay?" Jose moaned, trying to sit up.

"It's so cold in here!" Monica complained, her teeth chattering.

"Anybody up front awake yet!" Steve yelled loudly. Only a single soft crying sound could be heard. "Somebody had better get up there to see what's the matter," Steve said, in order motivate himself to stand up.

"Be careful, Steve," Maria cautioned. "You'd better crawl on your knees. The incline is too steep and you might slip back and dislodge the airplane from where it's sitting."

Steve just grunted in response to Maria's comment. He slowly unbuckled his seat belt and rolled out slowly on the floor of the airplane. Suddenly, the airplane shifted and the grinding of snow on the fuselage could be heard just for a moment and the jet could be felt moving slightly down the ridge. Steve froze, waiting for more movement. When none came, he relaxed slightly and began to crawl slowly up the incline toward the front of the cabin. By the time he reached the adults, the sun was entering the window, making it easier for him to see. He felt the carotid artery of each person.

"Only one has a pulse. I'm pretty sure the others are dead. They're blocking the way to the cockpit. If you want me to get there, I'm going to have to move one of them into her seat."

150

"Don't move anyone yet," Maria quickly responded. "Not until we see what's holding us here on the ridge."

The man who had come back to them and had threatened them was one of the dead. Steve's hands brushed the side of his suit coat as he turned around to return to his friends, and a small pile of important looking documents fell out. Steve reached for the documents and retrieved them, curious to see their contents. He opened them up and began reading. He frowned as he read and became angry as he finished the last document.

"You're not going to believe what I found. These guys aren't foreign agents who kidnapped us. They're our own people. President Ohm authorized them to kidnap us and to take us to a remote, secret air base in northern Chile and hold us hostage there to force Eclipse to give the United States the plans for the power source of the transporter."

"You're kidding!" Jose and Monica exclaimed simultaneously with surprise and animosity in their voices. They looked at each other in disbelief, becoming madder as each second passed.

"Jose, can you use your communicator?" asked Maria.

"Who could we call?" Jose said as he reached in his pocket and brought out the small, green crystal.

"Well, we can't call Tykesha and Summer. Their lives might be in danger. Amir might hurt them if he knows we're trying to reach them. It's got to be Eclipse. Somehow, maybe he could get here to save us. If we don't fall off this ridge and die, then we're going to freeze to death." Maria blew onto her right hand and then tried to warm her left hand by covering it with her right.

"But Eclipse won't come!" Jose exclaimed dejectedly.

"We can't give up, Jose! There's got to be a way out of here. We can't give up." Tears began to fill Maria's eyes as her voice began to fade out from hunger.

Jose put the communicator to his mouth and began to call Eclipse. Steve was carefully returning to the back of the cabin with his three friends. "Eclipse, this is Jose. We need your help. You're not going to believe us but it's true. The United States government kidnapped us. They wanted to do the same thing to us that Amir, the guy who has Summer and Tykesha, wants to do...to get the plans for

151

your power source. The US agents put us on this small jet and it crashed last night on the side of a tall, snow-covered ridge. All the agents are dead but one. It's really cold and if we don't get help soon, we'll die. Please help us Eclipse. Can you hear me?"

Everyone waited for the response. Suddenly, there was static and a voice started speaking. They all cheered as they recognized Eclipse. The static almost immediately increased, obscuring the entire message. They couldn't understand what he said!

"I'm not sure if it's better to know that he heard us; or not to know what he told us; or to have him make no response at all." Monica began to cry with hopelessness.

"Eclipse, this is Jose. Your entire message was covered by static. Can you repeat what you said again?"

Eclipse's voice came again, but again the static was too loud to decipher what he said.

"Eclipse, this is Jose. We still can't hear you. If you can hear us and understand what we said just say, Beep. If you couldn't understand us, say Bonk".

The youth listened intently. "Beep", they thought they could hear over the increased interference. Or was it "Bonk". No cheers were made. They had to be sure, but knew that there was no way to be sure now.

Steve was almost back to the rear of the cabin. The last time the jet shifted in the snow it became steeper, forcing Steve to hold onto the seats as he moved so that he wouldn't slide all the way to the back. He reached for an armrest of one of the seats but there was nothing there and he began to slide towards the rear of the airplane. He desperately grabbed for two more armrests but missed them. As he passed Jose, Jose grabbed him by the shirt. He suddenly came to a stop, but did not hit the back of the cabin. The change in momentum was enough to dislodge the airplane and it began to slide down the steep ridge.

The youth held their breaths. "Is it speeding up?" Monica cried.

"I think so," Steve yelled as he finally grabbed onto one of the seats and pulled himself back to his friends. "I'm sorry," he said as he wondered what would become of them now.

The airplane began to slide faster and then suddenly it came to

152

a stop. Instead of staying still, it began to teeter back and forth toward the back of the airplane as if that part were in mid-air. What they didn't know was that it had come to rest between the trunks of two small ancient pines that had begun to grow long ago but had died because of the extreme altitude. The pines were on the edge of a cliff. The tail portion of the airplane was over nothing but space-- a three thousand-foot drop to sharp rocks and sudden death. As the tail of the jet dipped down into space, the wings of the plane that were resting on the trunks came close to clearing them and plummeting to the rocks below.

"Based on the way this thing is rocking, I'd say we'd better quickly move to the front of the airplane," Steve said, beginning to pull himself back to the front of the cabin.

Jose was the next to go, then Monica and finally Maria. As they came closer to the front of the cabin, the rocking stopped and the jet rested firmly on the edge of the cliff.

"What does someone do when they have to go to the bathroom?" Jose asked, feeling extremely uncomfortable.

"Your in luck good buddy," Steve said, pointing to the door just to the right of the entrance to the cockpit. "All you have to do is to crawl over three dead United States agents." He felt the pulse of the one who was still alive. There was none. "Great, now there are four dead agents."

CHAPTER 11

The youth on the ridge were entering their third day in cabin temperatures between fifteen and twenty degrees. The smell of death was beginning to increase. Although they located blankets, there was no food on the airplane. A search of the cockpit for food had only revealed that the pilot and co-pilot also were dead. They began to sit two by two to take advantage of each others body heat in order to keep themselves from freezing. After looking under the lavatory washbasin they discovered a supply of water which had begun to freeze. They detached the portable jug and kept it moving to try to prevent it from freezing. They were grateful for this rare treasure, but their stomachs ached from hunger. When it looked like their efforts were failing and more and more of the water was freezing, they took turns putting the water jug under the blanket in between them.

The winds on the cliff were treacherous. At one point, they grabbed the tail of the jet and pushed it two or three inches off of the ground. The minutes seemed like hours and the hours like days. Their hope for survival began to disappear and they slept longer periods of time, not caring if they would wake up.

Summer and Tykesha had become extremely nervous. Each day, Amir had brought them out of Summer's room and had called Eclipse, breathing threats and telling him how long he had to get to them, before he killed Summer and Tykesha. Each time, his laugh became more fiendish. The General was constantly receiving instructions from the President of Iraq. Together, they were counting the hours before they had control over the entire world.

The morning of the seventh day came, each hour passing as fast as a snail crossing a sidewalk. Summer and Tykesha got up and looked at each other.

"Today's the day," Summer said quietly. I guess that Eclipse can't make it in time." Tykesha looked down, not knowing what to say. Summer hesitated and then continued. "Since we may die today, let's contact Steve and those guys."

"But Amir may see your communicator," Tykesha cautioned.

"When we're dead, we won't need the communicator anymore."

"Eclipse has to come!" Tykesha declared, not wanting to believe the ominous statement made by her friend.

Summer ignored Tykesha's comment and took out her communicator and put it close to her mouth. "Steve, come in, this is Summer." There was no response and Summer repeated her call, this time calling Maria's name first.

There were a few moments pause and Maria's voice could scarcely be heard from the communicator. "Hmmm, that's strange, there's no static. Why should her voice be so soft?" Summer immediately called again into her communicator. "Maria, this is Summer, repeat your message. We could hardly hear it. Why is your voice so weak?"

Maria's response was only a little louder and the girls strained to hear every word. "Summer, thank God you called."

A feeling of panic filled Summer's heart. "What's the matter, Maria?"

Another short pause occurred. This time Maria's voice was a little stronger. "We were kidnapped by United States agents pretending to be agents of another country. They wanted to use us as hostages to get Eclipse to give them the secret of his power. Then, the airplane they took us in crashed on a real tall mountain. Oh, Summer, I think we're going to freeze to death!" There was a long pause as the sobbing of Maria could be heard. She finally stopped long enough to continue. "I can't wake up Monica and Steve..... bu..but I think they're still breathing. Jose is trying hard to stay awake. If you hadn't of called me I would have fallen asleep. I just can't stay awake for long periods of time any longer." The feeling of surrender filled her last comment.

Tears swelled up in Tykesha's and Summer's eyes. Maria's dismal report filled them with fear. They felt helpless. They were angry with the governments of Iraq and the United States for using them as pawns in a game of international power. They felt sick at the possibility of losing their best friends in the whole world... or universe. Summer elected not to tell Maria of their impending death that day if Eclipse did not return.

156

"Maria, you've got to hang on. You can do it! You can do it!" Tykesha also called words of encouragement to their friend. They were about to continue their conversation when they heard the huge lock being loosened at their door.

"Call you later Maria," Summer whispered breathlessly. She quickly placed the communicator back into her pocket. She was sure that they had been detected and would be severely punished or even tortured.

Suddenly the door swung quickly open and Amir and three armed guards were standing in the doorway. Summer and Tykesha gulped, not moving an inch. The four men came quickly into the room and walked up to the two girls as they sat, motionless, on the bed.

"You are eight hours from dying!" declared Amir, his eyes filled with a mixture of emotions. His major fear was that Eclipse would not come. He could see his plans for world domination vaporizing into the air. Inussein's son, now the supreme ruler of Iraq, had promised him that he would be elevated to second in power. The possible loss of this honor filled him with rage and frustration. He wanted to put more pressure on Eclipse in an effort to force him to come. So great was his focus on this quest for power that he had not paid any attention to his surveillance cameras that watched every corner of Summer's room.

Amir commanded the girls to get up and pointed toward the door. Tykesha and Summer looked at each other, giving a secret sigh of relief at not having been discovered. Now, they were curious about where they were being taken. They walked through a series of dark hallways, finally emerging at the office that Summer had first been taken to after she arrived in Baghdad. Two of the guards placed blindfolds over the girls' eyes and escorted them out of the door to a waiting limousine. Once inside, with one guard in the front seat and Amir with the other two guards on the seat facing Summer and Tykesha, the car drove to the exit of the mountain fortress and waited as the huge door moved open. The car emerged into the hot morning sun and drove quickly back to Baghdad.

An air of secrecy surrounded the limousine as it entered a back gate of the new Imperial Palace in the heart of the city. Amir was not about to expose his plans to the Iraqi press and especially not to the international press. He had seen what it had done to embarrass the President of the United States and the commander of Bill Air Force Base and he was making sure that the same embarrassment did not come to him, or to Inussein's son. The limousine turned into the underground parking garage, passing the nine foot, solid, reinforced titanium wall that surrounded the entire palace, making it impregnable to missile attack.

The limousine came to a stop in one of a dozen empty parking spaces and the girls were escorted into the building. It was not until they came to the Washington D.C. equivalent to the Oval Office that their blindfolds were removed. They were invited to sit down. The three guards covered each of the doors and Amir waited, pacing back and forth in front of the President's desk. After a few minutes, Inussein himself came into the room. He strutted across the floor and walked up to the girls.

"Welcome to my palace." He reached his hand out to the girls. Summer wanted to spit on his hand but decided that it wouldn't help the situation at all. She stood up and politely shook hands. Tykesha quickly followed Summer's example.

"I trust that you have been treated well by Amir?"

Amir tensed and glared at the girls. They noticed his menacing look out of the corners of their eyes and nodded their heads, mechanically. Amir relaxed and smiled. Inussein walked over to his desk and sat down. "Well, General Kasafuut, show me this communicator that you have that can talk to the alien, Eclipse."

Amir took the small, green crystal and handed it the President. Inussein looked surprised and then skeptical. "Surely, General you don't expect me to believe that this small, green crystal has the capability to communicate across the entire universe?"

"I was as skeptical as you, until Summer showed me how powerful it was."

Inussein looked at Summer and then back at Amir. "Did she communicate to the alien?"

"No sir. To her friends in the United States, who also possess a similar communicator."

Inussein stood up, walked around his desk to the luxurious

couch where Summer and Tykesha were sitting and looked intently at his visitors. "Can one of you young ladies show me how this works?"

Tykesha was the first to respond. Inussein placed the communicator into her hand and Tykesha placed it close to her mouth and began speaking. "Maria, this is Tykesha. We are in the office of the President Inussein, the leader of Iraq. He wants to hear your voice so he knows that this communicator works." She stopped talking and looked at Summer as they all waited for a response. Summer gave her a look of approval for the way in which she handled the tense situation.

Suddenly, Maria's voice was heard clearly from the crystalline device. It was obvious that she was forcing herself to talk as loudly as she could and was trying not to reveal that they had talked only a short time before. "I can read you loud and clear Tykesha. How's things going there?"

"Everything is about as good as can be expected, Maria. I've got to go now. Hope to talk to you later."

"Hope to see you soon my friends," Maria responded.

Tykesha handed the communicator back to Inussein, trying to hide the tears that were creeping into the corner of her eyes. The President handed the communicator to Amir, impressed at the demonstration of the power of the device. Amir then placed the communicator close to his mouth. "Eclipse, this is General Amir Kasafuut. Summer and Tykesha and I are in the Imperial Palace of the President of Iraq in Baghdad. We expect you to be here no later than seven hours from now. If you do not come, we will kill your friends."

There was no response. "Why didn't he answer your call, Amir?" Inussein questioned.

"He hasn't responded to any of my requests." Then, looking at the girls, Amir said, "It looks like he is no friend of yours. You help him save his planet and how does he repay you? He allows you to be killed. I would not like to have a friend like that."

Summer could no longer hold her tongue. She jumped to her feet and yelled at the General. "How dare you criticize our friend! He will come, just you wait and see!" The guards pointed their rifles

159

at Summer and began stepping toward her. After a moment, she calmed down enough to return to her seat. The ticking of the grandfather clock in Inussein's office pounded in their ears, making the time pass by much more slowly. Inussein left his office to attend to his other duties of state while the small group waited, becoming more nervous as the minutes passed.

"Eclipse, this is General Kasafuut again. You now have only six hours before your friends are killed. It looks to me like you are not a friend at all but care only about your planet. You must give us the ability to create the power source of your ship on the earth. This will allow us to spare the lives of your friends."

"Eclipse, this is the General. There are only five hours. My guards are getting ready to exterminate Summer and Tykesha."

"Eclipse, this is the General once again. If you are playing a game, it will not go well for your friends. You have only four hours remaining to come to this palace and give us the information that we demand."

"Eclipse, this is General Kasafuut. You only have three hours left." The General looked at his watch. The communicator was as silent as it had always been. Inussein came into his office and looked at Amir. "Nothing yet, my President. But rest assured that this fellow Eclipse will be here and he will give us what we want."

"You had better be right, Amir. I am getting very impatient. If this alien does not come and give us the ability to create an unlimited power source, then you will no longer be my Minister of Defense." Inussein turned and left his office. A dark cloud of tension continued to increase in the room.

Amir gulped. The last Minister of Defense was killed in front of a firing squad when he had displeased Inussein. He wondered what he could do that might allow him to get a response from Eclipse. As he thought, an idea suddenly came to him. He turned and looked at the girls and laughed silently to himself.

When the next announcement to Eclipse was due, Amir walked up to Summer and handed the communicator to her. "You call and tell Eclipse that he has two hours to get here."

Summer slowly took the green, crystal communicator from Amir. She looked at the grandfather clock. At five o'clock in the

160

afternoon, she would no longer be alive. Eclipse had to come... he just had to. "Eclipse, this is Summer. The General asked me to tell you that we have two hours before they kill us. I want you to know, my friend, that we have never doubted your friendshi....."

Amir grabbed the communicator from Summer and put it to his mouth. "They do doubt your friendship, Eclipse. I can see it in their eyes as they get closer to death." He angrily put the communicator into his pocket. When no response came to Summer's voice, he became extremely nervous, frantically pacing around the office. Within two hours, he would be forced to kill the girls and then he would suffer death at the hands of the firing squad.

Inussein and several of his deputies entered the room. He was obviously irritated at the wait and briskly walked up to his desk. He sat down and stared coolly at Amir. "I see no alien yet, Amir."

"He will come, sir." Amir put the communicator close to his mouth. "Eclipse, this is Amir Kasafuut. You have only one hour left. I see great doubt in the eyes of your friends, Summer and Tykesha. The doubt that is within them is growing by the minute. They will die unless you come and give us the information."

"It's not true!" Tykesha yelled, jumping up and lunging at Amir. Amir nodded to the guard closest to her. "We know if you don't come, Eclipse, that it's because..."

The guard hit Tykesha's face just before she reached the general, silencing her. She covered her face and began to cry. Summer came to her side and put her arms around her friend as if to protect her. At gunpoint, the girls were forced to sit down on the couch.

CHAPTER 12

The sudden movement of the jet caused Maria and Jose to wake up. Monica and Steve, who were sitting next to each other, did not awaken. They lay still, their bodies appearing to be without life.

"What happened?" Jose questioned groggily.

"I don't know," Maria said, frightened at the sudden movement of the airplane.

Suddenly a cracking sound came from the outside where the wing of the aircraft was caught on the tree. The jet slipped closer to the edge of the cliff. The wind raced around the jet, causing it to rise and fall in a seesaw-like motion. Maria was closest to the window and leaned carefully to look outside. The morning sun was just coming up. She saw the cliff and the drop-off below the airplane. She also saw a large crack in the old tree. As she leaned closer to look, the jet wing lowered over the side of the tree. Maria quickly moved back toward Jose and the jet wing came back up. Jose wanted to scream but could not speak.

"Oh no!" cried Maria. She could see her breath as she spoke. "I think the tree out there is breaking and we're at the edge of a cliff. We're going to fall off!"

She looked to the other side where Monica and Steve lay, motionless. "Maybe we can move to the other side and take some of the weight of the jet off of that tree."

Jose was the first to move across the isle and sit in the seat in front of Monica and Steve. The jet didn't move. Maria was the next to move. She brought the blanket with her and they covered themselves with it. Nothing happened and they breathed a sigh of relief. They fastened their seat belts and looked at the sun entering the window. Maria looked at her watch. "It's been almost seven hours since Tykesha called us from Iraq. I wish we could call them but it might put their lives in danger." She did not realize that at that same moment, Amir had just ordered his guards to take Summer and Tykesha to a special room in the palace in order to kill them. A huge wind came from the side of the plane where the four youth sat. The jet began to slide toward the abyss below. It stopped. Again,

Jose and Maria held their breath. Then a decisive crack occurred and they became weightless and the jet began to fall toward the rocks several thousand feet below. Maria screamed and Jose yelled in fear. They had come to the end of their lives. They lost consciousness.

The transporter suddenly appeared from behind an isolated group of cirrus clouds and a beam of light shot down from the transporter and engulfed the falling jet. Somehow this beam halted its fall and the light acted like a string, dangling its cargo at the end. The transporter edged toward an unpopulated wilderness valley at eight thousand feet and gently allowed the jet to rest on the ground. The beam changed colors and the four youth were drawn up into the medical facility of the transporter. Eclipse activated the invisibility device and the transporter disappeared as it sped toward Baghdad.

Tykesha and Summer walked out of Inussein's office, followed by Amir and the three guards with their rifles pointing toward the girls. Amir was upset. He had seen the look of disappointment in Inussein's eyes and knew that he had already decided to replace him as Minister of Defense. They hadn't walked five yards when the afternoon sun that was shining into a tiny window at the end of the hallway suddenly disappeared. Then it quickly grew darker, as if huge clouds had covered the entire sky. The small group stopped at the elevators and Amir told them to wait. They watched him walk to the end of the hallway and stare out of the window. At that moment, lightning began to come down from the huge, ominous dark thunderclouds. Large claps of thunder came immediately after each lightning bolt and shook the palace and the other buildings of the city. Dark clouds covered the entire city of Baghdad. Amir could see that the lightning bolts occasionally hit several of the smaller buildings around them. In some, fires had begun. The people on the streets of Baghdad had been frightened by the mysterious appearance of the thunderclouds and by the unleashed lightning and deafening thunder that had followed. They ran from the streets and took shelter inside the buildings nearest them. A large bolt of lightning struck the top of the palace, the tallest building in Baghdad. Inussein and his deputies had also rushed to the tiny window in his office and were looking at nature's display of power.

The lights of the palace began to flicker on and off. The automatic alarms began to sound and the small windows were covered by thick titanium metal. Another flash of lightning hit the palace and then another. Inussein felt like they were under attack. Each time lightning struck the top of the palace, a strong charge of static electricity covered the entire outside surface of the building.

Amir was frightened as the lightning struck the palace. Each time, he felt the hair on his body stand up. He ran to the emergency exit and touched the ornamental metallic door to push it open. A huge flash of static electricity passed from the door to his finger. He cried in pain as the force of the shock pushed him off of his feet and onto the floor. The three guards did not dare get close to him. They had felt the large electrical charge transferred to the building and feared the same fate if they touched Amir. The cry had alerted Inussein and his deputies and they came running out into the hall to see Amir laying, whimpering on the floor.

"Quick!" commanded Inussein. "Turn on the outside monitors so we can see what's happening!" His deputies disappeared into his office and turned on a console behind a false wall, containing seven television monitors. The others, including Summer and Tykesha, rushed into the room to see what was happening, leaving Amir on the floor to nurse his own pain. They hadn't felt a charge of static electricity that strong since the appearance of the strange light on the ridge, in what seemed to them, hundreds of years ago. Could it be Eclipse? Had he made it? Oh, please, let it be Eclipse, the girls thought to themselves.

As Tykesha and Summer entered the room they saw the events occurring on the different monitors. The lightning was no longer striking the buildings of the city but was hitting only the palace. They could see the fearful inhabitants of Baghdad peer out of the windows of the neighboring buildings around them as they watched lightning bolt after lightning bolt hit the palace. Some even ventured out of the buildings to get a better look. Each time the lightning hit, the hairs on the bodies of all the palace occupants stood up on end. No one dared touch anything or anyone near them.

Suddenly, the people in the streets screamed and ran toward the safety of the buildings near them and all the curious onlookers from the windows disappeared. Inussein was searching the monitors to try to find the reason for their change in behavior. The middle monitor answered his silent question. It was a full view of the palace from a television camera on a building three hundred yards distant.

"Look, look!" Inussein exclaimed to his deputies in his foreign tongue. "The cloud above the palace is changing..."

Even Summer and Tykesha saw what was happening. The cloud was beginning to take the form of... they held their breath recognizing what seemed to them to be very similar to the transporter. The lightning had completely stopped. Within a minute the change was complete. "Eclipse!" Summer and Tykesha declared almost in unison.

Inussein started to turn around to order the guards to hold the girls. He was suddenly interrupted by the other men who had not taken their eyes off of the central monitor. A beam of light was extending from the transporter to the top of the palace. Smoke was coming from the metallic titanium shield. Then they could see liquid titanium flowing off of the sides of the building. The beam was literally melting its way through the titanium wall. A series of crashes occurred directly above Inussein's office and the ceiling collapsed and fell to the floor. The beam of light shone on the floor. Inussein and his men whirled around when the noise occurred and stared in horror as they watched the form of some kind of monster begin to appear. Tykesha and Summer immediately recognized the "disguised" form of Eclipse but pretended that they were as scared as the others in the room and they backed away. The monster was now in full view, and as they backed up, the girls winked so that Eclipse would know that they recognized him. The monster roared and advanced toward Inussein and his men, who stood frozen from fear. The green slime covered the floor of Inussein's office.

"Quick!" yelled Tykesha, thinking quickly. "That's not Eclipse, it's a monster from the planet we went to. He probably attacked and killed our friend." The monster towered over the men and roared and writhed back and forth. Some of the men began to vomit as they saw the worm-like creatures moving about the monster's body.

"Don't let it touch you. You'll get a horrible disease and die a slow, painful death." Tykesha controlled the laughter that was

166

coming from within.

That was all the encouragement the men needed. They quickly ran, avoiding the advance of the monster and left the room. Eclipse turned around and went into the light, motioning for the girls to get into the light with him. As the three of them entered the light, they disappeared and reappeared in the main control room of the transporter.

When they reappeared, Eclipse was in his real form and they ran and hugged him. "Eclipse! Boy, are you a sight for sore eyes!" Tears flowed freely.

"Eclipse, Maria and the rest of them are going to die on a tall mountain. We've got to get there quick!"

Eclipse looked at Summer and smiled. "They are okay. They are in the medical facility and sleeping peacefully. Once I saved them, I came immediately to you and have not had time to treat them. Let us get out of the earth's atmosphere and take care of your friends. Then I have some business that needs to be finished in your country." His eyes twinkled with mischief during his final statement to the girls. He turned and spoke commands to the computer and the light in between the transporter and the palace disappeared. He activated the invisibility device and the transporter disappeared from before the view of the few courageous, but skeptical onlookers of the events of those few minutes.

When they were safely out of the atmosphere of the earth, they moved quickly to the medical facility. As they walked through the metallic-like door, they were met with a temperature of almost ninety degrees and their four friends laying on the top of the medical examination tables. Eclipse spoke a command to the medical computer and the temperature decreased.

"Even though I didn't have time to see them, the computer sensed that they were almost completely frozen, so the temperature was automatically adjusted," Eclipse explained.

"Eclipse, do the rays from the communicator travel at the speed of light or beyond the speed of light?" Summer interrupted as if she hadn't even heard what Eclipse had said.

Eclipse smiled and looked at Summer with fondness. "They go much faster than the speed of light, Summer."

167

Summer was content with the quick answer, so she turned her attention to her four friends. Tykesha was already by Monica, trying to wake her up and Summer went directly to Steve. She glanced and saw Maria and Jose beginning to wake up, so she grabbed Steve by the shoulder and began to shake him. "Wake up Steve. It's okay. We're back on the transporter."

Neither Steve nor Monica responded to the sound of the girls' voices. They looked worried. "Are they dead?" Tykesha asked.

"No, Tykesha. They are in a deep sleep." He moved over to another part of the medical room and activated a machine which moved over each of the sleeping youth. A buzzing sounded as the machine came over Steve and Monica's heads. After a few minutes, they began to wake up. Soon, the six friends were hugging each other, rapidly explaining all that had happened to them. Eclipse excused himself and disappeared for a few moments. He reappeared with a large tray of fluids and solid looking multi-colored objects of food that the youth immediately recognized and began to devour with enthusiasm. Eclipse stood happily watching the familiar faces of his friends.

"Eclipse, did you save your planet and family?" Summer asked in the middle of a bite of a purple object that tasted like chicken.

"Yes, Summer, thanks to you and your friends my planet is going to do well and my people are a lot wiser."

"Eclipse, why couldn't we hear you when we called you from the jet?" Maria drank the last drop of the yellow fluid in her glass as she asked the question.

"Almost immediately after receiving Summer's first call for help, I began one of the quickest trips through the universe taken by a human form. The computer of the transporter was able to clarify your messages to me but your communicators are not equipped to make my messages clear to you when I am moving above the speed of light."

Eclipse looked at his friends to see if they understood. He could tell by the looks in their eyes that they had comprehended what he had told them. "Now it is time to go to the United States before we return you to your own time. I need to visit three people." Eclipse walked through the door and headed toward the main control room of the transporter while Summer and her friends followed closely behind, curious about who he was about to visit.

When they entered the control room, Eclipse asked them to sit in the seats that were very familiar to them by now. He turned to the crystalline screen and the shape of the entire earth filled the huge screen. He spoke commands to the computer and they quickly approached the North American continent.

As they got closer to the United States, Steve exclaimed, "Why are we going to the East Coast?"

"The United States has a President there that cares more about power than about his people and of the plight of a world depleted of its natural oil resources." Eclipse became silent and the six youth looked at the crystalline screen, wondering what would happen next. To their surprise, they recognized the city of Washington D.C. and, in particular, the White House, growing larger and larger on the crystalline viewer. Soon they were only twenty or thirty yards above the beautiful building. He spoke a command and an object that looked like a large compact disc was automatically fed into a strange-looking machine. Suddenly a news reporter appeared on the screen and began giving part of the news.

"Is this coming from that big CD, Eclipse?" Monica asked.

"Yes, but wait The best part is coming. This broadcast is replacing the real one that the President is listening to as well as the one everyone else in the world is watching. In fact, it is now being permanently replaced on the current tapes of the CNV network." Eclipse's eyes sparkled with anticipation.

"And now, we interrupt this CNV report to bring to our viewers around the world a CNV special report. President Ohm, the President of the United States of America, authorized the kidnapping of four youth from his own country that had claimed to travel beyond the speed of light. His purpose was to force the alien with whom the youth traveled to give the United States Government the secrets of the power of his space ship to solve the country's energy problems and to use it to control the world. His plan backfired when the jet in which the abducted youth were traveling crashed in the mountains of Peru, killing all agents and the pilots. The youth miraculously survived."

169

President Ohm stared in disbelief at the news summary he was viewing. His entire family was there with him, watching the report. His face became red from embarrassment as his children and wife glared at him with disgust. Congressional leaders who were watching the broadcast had finally found the weakness that they needed to begin impeachment proceedings.

"Meanwhile in Iraq," the report continued, "we have actual tapes of what happened to Inussein's Imperial Palace today as a result of his kidnapping of two other American youth who reportedly were on the same journey beyond the speed of light." The crystalline screen showed the lightning coming down from the sky and pounding the palace repeatedly. It also showed the beam of light melting a hole through the thick titanium metal but did not show the form of the transporter.

"Inussein's plan was the same as that of the President of the United States," the reporter continued. "The two youth, however, are now safe and heading toward the United States. Our Iraqi correspondent has just notified us that the private office of Inussein has been permanently sealed off from the world. A new office for the Iraqi President is currently being planned in the west wing of the palace."

President Ohm's face was covered with sweat. He left the room. Suddenly, the darkness outside was brightly illuminated by multiple bolts of lightning coming from thick clouds, directly over the White House. He looked out of the window and was startled to see the lightning strike the trees, grass and shrubbery all around the grounds. Each time it struck, holes were placed in the lawn, trees split in two, crashing to the earth, and flower beds were demolished. Loud claps of thunder caused the White House to shake and move, almost as if an earthquake had occurred. After only sixty seconds, the grounds of the White House were almost completely destroyed. It looked like it had been attacked by terrorists. The White House security force, momentarily frozen by the violence of the lightning and thunder, rapidly exited their posts, ready to fire on any intruder. As they looked into the heavens, they saw the clouds dissipate and finally disappear. There was no foe…there was no intruder. The calm of the cool October evening had returned. They stood,

170

speechless, looking at each other in dismay and examining the destruction in disbelief.

The transporter left the East Coast and quickly traveled west. Within seconds they were above Utah and descending. The youth recognized Bill Air Force Base. Then the crystalline screen switched to the room with the pine tree in it. The six teenagers realized just how mad Eclipse was and how much he had been angered at the treatment that they had received from those that should have been protecting them. They watched carefully as he deactivated the invisibility device and activated two beams of light. Suddenly, General Lever and the Colonel appeared in the room. The invisibility device was activated once again. Eclipse disappeared through the door as he was transforming himself back into the form of the monster. They could hardly wait to see what he might do with these two men who had caused so much pain and difficulty for them.

General Lever looked around him and was surprised to see the Colonel beside him. "Ho..How did we get here?" General Lever asked. Then, as he looked around the room, horror filled his heart as he recognized the room that he had seen on the video, taken by the probe over twenty-one years ago.

"General, isn't this the same room we saw in the classified video two weeks ago?" The Colonel's voice quivered with nervousness as the General nodded. The Colonel gulped. "The one with the m..monster?" Again the General nodded, annoyed at the question. The two men began to panic and they quickly covered the entire room, feeling the metallic walls to see if they could find a way out. There was no escape. They sweated profusely as the monitors disappeared and the shape of a door appeared.

Summer and her friends were beginning to cheer. They saw Eclipse, his monster, bloody teeth sparkling in the light, pass through the door. The youth had recalled how frightened they had been in their first encounter with their friend. As the two men dropped to their knees, screaming and pleading with the monster for their lives, the youth cheered again. The men screamed louder as he came near, roaring in anger. They finally saw the worm-like hairs of his body continually moving and the green slime underneath him.

They covered their eyes and buried their heads on the floor, so they could not see the monster any more.

"Why do you invade my ship!" Eclipse cried out in a frightening voice that the youth had never heard him use before.

"We didn't invade your ship. We don't even know how we got here," the General responded, his voice shaky from the fear that gripped his heart. He refused to look at the monster.

"Why did you shoot my friend, Steve, and treat my other friends so badly? Why did you treat them like prisoners of war?" The Colonel and General could not speak. They only hoped that their death would be quick and painless. But nothing happened. Instead, their worst nightmare began to unfold.

"I will be watching you every day and every night," hissed the horrible voice of the monster. "There is nowhere you can go to hide from me." The men began to cry. "If you treat any other human being like you treated my friends, then I shall come to you and your fate will be in my hands. You will never know around what corner I will be found or in what building you will discover me or if I will come into your home with your families. Remember, I will be watching your every move, listening to every thought you think and every word you speak."

The men became so frightened they passed out and became limp. Eclipse turned and went through the door once again. Summer and her friends were happy and sad at the same time. Somehow they felt sorry for these two men who lay on the floor, but they were happy with the way Eclipse had frightened them into not treating others unkindly. They watched as the invisibility device was deactivated automatically and the two men slowly disappear. The device activated automatically as Eclipse came through the door, smiling.

"Where did they go," asked Monica in wonderment.

"Back to where we picked them up on the base," Eclipse declared in victory.

"I'm sure glad we're your friends, Eclipse," Jose commented, laughing. The others broke the tension with laughter.

"It is now time to return you to your original time." Eclipse looked sad and so did the teenagers. This would probably be the last time they would see each other.

"I'm scared, Eclipse," Maria said shakily. "If we go back to our time, we probably will get the same treatment that we just did." The others nodded their heads in agreement. Maria continued. "I don't want to be some scientific curiosity, studied and guarded or kidnapped by others wanting to know your secrets."

"I'm afraid to go back, too," Steve added, remembering the pain of his visit to Bill Air Force Base. "Couldn't we go with you to your planet?"

"There is a way, my friends, that you can live in your time without being examined." The teenagers crowded closer to him, waiting for his response. "I believe that I can return you to precisely the time before Summer's father and the National Guard arrived." Eclipse then went on to explain the rest of his plan.

CHAPTER 13

"It is now time," Eclipse said, looking wistfully at his six friends. "Please go into your quarters and lay down. The speeds that we will be going require you to be completely still and in a relaxed, reclined position."

The youth obeyed and went to their quarters and lay down on their beds. They were exhausted from their trials and stresses that they had passed through and they quickly fell asleep. After insuring that they were asleep, Eclipse began to accelerate to speeds well beyond the speed of light. The stars on the crystalline viewer blurred and then reversed direction. Multi-colored lights appeared and disappeared as his speed continued to increase. Suddenly, all light disappeared from view on the crystalline screen and Eclipse spoke a command to his computer. Digital numbers, counting the seconds appeared on the control panel. One, two, three...twenty-five, twenty-six, twenty-seven. At thirty seconds, the lights of the stars reappeared and the transporter began slowing as it approached the planet earth.

Eclipse went into the rooms where the youth still lay, sleeping soundly. He hated to disturb them but knew that it was now time for them to return to their homes and families. How he had wanted them to come to his planet and live with his family! But he knew the sadness it would bring to their families on earth. Each of the teenagers groaned as they were awakened. Once they realized where they were, they quickly got up and accompanied their friend into the main control room.

"Are we back to our own time, Eclipse?" Summer questioned.

"Yes."

"But its all dark!" Jose complained. "Couldn't we..."

"Do you see this small circle of lights at the entrance of Lambs Canyon?" A small blinking light appeared on the viewer to indicate the spot. The youth tried to see the detail of area, but were unsuccessful. Eclipse spoke a command to the computer and that tiny area was enlarged to the entire screen.

"There's my dad and Doug Volcano! They sure look young!" Summer almost jumped up and down with the joy she felt at seeing her father as she remembered him on the day that they left for their hike to the top of Mt. Walamalee.

"They are just now meeting with the National Guard to come up to the ridge. By the time you leave the transporter and hike back down from the ridge, you will meet them in your original camping area. Remember what we discussed." The youth looked at Eclipse and nodded their heads. "I will give you one flashlight to allow you to see the trail, but you must dispose of the light before you meet anyone. Also, please give me your communicators. I want to be able to talk to you, but if anyone found out what they really are, your troubles would begin again."

All but Tykesha's was returned. Although Amir still had Tykesha's, Eclipse had inactivated it electronically prior to their leaving the palace. They knew that they would never be able to contact Eclipse again during their lives. The invisibility device was deactivated and the transporter gently landed on the ridge. Eclipse accompanied the youth to the room with the pine tree and the outer door of the transporter automatically opened. The six teenagers stood there, tears coming to their eyes. Eclipse was trying to hold back his emotions but a tear, trickling down his cheek, betrayed his attempt. Summer ran and gave Eclipse a hug, followed by her friends. As they passed by the pine tree they touched its branches and it seemed to respond to each of their touches.

"Good bye, my friends. Thank you for the sacrifices you have made." He watched them disappear into the darkness and walk down the trail. The door to the transporter slowly closed and then the transporter itself became invisible. It slowly took off, gaining speed as it left the atmosphere of the earth.

The six teenagers neared the meadow. The moonlight made it appear like a silver fairyland. On the other side of the meadow, they saw the flashlights of the men and women of the National Guard as they were preparing their equipment for transport to the ridge. Summer turned off the flashlight and quickly threw it deeper into the forest. They came into full view in the meadow and began to increase their pace as they walked toward the lights in front of them. It wasn't long before they neared the group of men.

"Daddy!" Summer called in a loud voice.

176

Suddenly the talking among the men stopped. Summer called again. "Daddy, its me, Summer!"

"Summer!" yelled Tom Solstice. "Is it really you?" The small group of teenagers approached the National Guard. The flashlights of the men were all turned toward them.

"Oh God. Thank you!" Mr. Solstice cried out loudly. He began sobbing as he ran toward his daughter. They met half way and embraced. Time was suspended for that moment.

Doug Volcano walked up quickly behind them and saw the five Freshman he had witnessed disappear into the light only hours before. He stared as if he had seen a ghost. Mr. Solstice's friend, Dr. Winter, from Utah State University, came running up. By this time all of the teenagers were in a tight circle around Mr. Solstice and Doug.

"What happened to you. Each of you disappeared into a mysterious light?" Dr. Winter exclaimed with curiosity.

Summer took a deep breath, remembering what Eclipse had told them and hoped that their plan would work. "Well, it was really the coolest thing that's ever happened to me. When I walked into the light, I walked out of an identical light, onto the top of another ridge about two or three miles from where I entered. It was real scary. I didn't know where I was, so, just like you taught me, Dad, I stayed where I was so someone could find me. I was really happy when I saw another light appear and out came these guys." Summer pointed to her friends. "We decided to hike back together and try to find the ridge. It took us a while, but we finally got there earlier tonight. We were going to sleep on top of the ridge, but it got a little cold, so we woke up about midnight and decided to walk down here."

Dr. Winter was dumbfounded. "Is that what happened to you, also?" he skeptically asked Summer's friends.

"Yes sir," Steve said confidently. "None of us can explain it, but you can be sure that we're not going to walk into any more lights on mountain ridges... are we Summer?"

Summer shook her head dramatically. "It certainly cured my curious streak," Summer affirmed. The others nodded and looked at the expression of Dr. Winter. He shook his head and thought for a minute.

"I'd better contact NASA and have them cancel the special investigation team." He turned around and got into his car and used his cellular telephone.

"Welcome to science class, students. My name is Mr. Quake and we're going to learn a lot this first eight weeks about our solar system and the universe. We know a lot about our own solar system, thanks to the space probes that have been sent out by various nations. But beyond that, it is only speculation to what we will find or if there is life on other planets in other galaxies like our own. No human has ever traveled beyond our moon. They would die, traveling to the galaxy nearest us..."

Summer looked and smiled at Tykesha, Steve, Monica, Jose and Maria who also smiled about the comment that their science teacher had just made during the first period science class of their freshman year. Although they wanted to raise their hands and tell the class what it was really like traveling through the universe at much greater than the speed of light, they realized that they would never be able to tell their story. It was worth it, for they now felt safe from those who desired power, safe in their own homes, together with their own family and friends. They turned their thoughts from their teachers's lecture to the future state of planet earth, depleted of all its oil resources. Would it really happen? Could they do anything to change that condition? Imagination carried them on the future journey of their life that was now full of hope and promise.

About the Author

Dr. Taylor was a medical researcher for almost eleven years and then entered the teaching profession as a high school science teacher for the next eleven years. It was during the latter part of his time as a teacher that he began writing adventure stories to help his Chemistry and Earth and Physical Science students understand and appreciate the excitement and daily application of science. "The Disappearance of Summer Solstice" is the second in the series of those works.